PUFFIN BOOKS

Editor: Kaye Webb

TO THE WILD SKY

Everyone was waiting for the engine to stop. It was
bound to run out of fuel some time. The six children
seemed to have been sitting in this plane, imprisoned,
for days, waiting to die. And Gerald, who had taken
over the controls when disaster struck their pilot, just
flew on and on, almost as though he didn't know how
to go down. Tomorrow was his fourteenth birthday,
but he hadn't much hope of seeing it.

And if they did land, where would it be? On the
mountains? On the sea? Somewhere near habitation,
or in the desert wastes or even in New Guinea, where
the savages were? It would take a miracle now to save
the party who had set off that Friday afternoon to visit
a sheep station in New South Wales.

Four boys and two girls, six different people, how
would they stand up to this terrifying situation? Who
would be a good leader, and who would crack under
the strain? Would they work as a group, or would their
disagreements kill them all? Ivan Southall, author of
Hills End and *Ash Road*, already has a reputation for
his character studies of children in danger, which this
book can only enhance.

For readers of eleven and over.

To the Wild Sky won the Australian Children's
Book of the Year Award for 1968.

Cover design by Elisabeth Grant

Ivan Southall

To the Wild Sky
Illustrated by Jennifer Tuckwell

Penguin Books

Penguin Books Ltd, Harmondsworth,
Middlesex, England
Penguin Books Australia Ltd, Ringwood,
Victoria, Australia

First published by Angus & Robertson 1967
Published in Puffin Books 1971
Copyright © Ivan Southall 1967

Made and printed in Australia by The Dominion Press,
North Blackburn, Victoria
Set in Linotype Baskerville

Contents

1. Bert

The *Egret* – she was rugged rather than beautiful – thudded down on the landing strip beside Lake Ooleroo shortly after midday.

Jim Butler put her down like a ton of bricks – as pilots went he, too, was sometimes rugged rather than beautiful when no one was there to watch – but she could take it; she was used to rough strips and treacherous clay-pans and rock-hard plains. Her designer had intended her for the bush. One thing was sure: had she been able to make her voice heard she would have protested bitterly about the name they had painted on her side. '*Egret?*' she might well have said, 'am I a spindly bird? Am I adorned in fine plumes? Am I a pretty, prancing thing?'

She was early and the children who were to fill her up were not due until one-fifteen. Jim Butler had reckoned on strong head winds – Hennessy had warned him that they were a certainty – but they hadn't happened, so now he was left with about an hour to kill; too short a time to ring for a taxi and run into town for lunch; too long a time to sit and merely think.

Jim was an energetic man, a busy sort of man, the sort of man who found it difficult to do nothing, so he walked over to the phone box that was attached to the windsock mast and rang through to the agent at the oil depot. 'How are you set for aviation fuel?' he said.

'O.K.,' said the agent.

'I'm out on the strip. Can you top up my tanks? Say thirty gallons.'

'Sure. Who for?'

'Hennessy. The Coonabibba Hennessys. Are they good for credit with you?'

'Credit! Don't you carry that much with you?'

'Never,' said Jim, 'on principle. Do you give credit or don't you?'

'Sure. Hennessy's good with me at any time, though we haven't done business for a while. How come he's not flying it himself?'

'I haven't pinched it, mate,' sighed Jim, 'if that's what you mean.' It was a question he had tired of. He had met it of late in a dozen mid-western towns. 'The name's Butler. I've been flying for Hennessy since his horse threw him. Or hadn't you heard?'

'Hennessy's big in his way, Mr Butler, but he's not national news, is he?' However, the agent must have been satisfied, for he said, 'That crate holds more than thirty gallons, you know.'

'I know, mate! I know how much she'll take to top her up.'

Jim banged the receiver down, paced back to the aircraft, and wondered why he was so irritable, so unusually restless. If he had known why, he might have gone into town and had that lunch, but he would hardly have bothered about extra fuel. On the other hand ... but it is difficult to predict what he might have done. It is just as well that the future is hidden from men.

Mark was at the window with the curtains held back, waiting impatiently for the car; his mother's voice, nagging at him from the background, was a sound he scarcely bothered to listen to. He knew quite well what she would be saying, because she had already said it a dozen times. Colin was listening, anyway. Colin was like that. He always managed to wear a look that expressed the proper degree of attention. Even Mark appreciated that Colin was the type of boy grown-ups liked.

'When you get to Coonabibba,' Mrs Kerr was saying, 'you are to remember that you are guests. Particularly you, Mark. You are to remember that you are not in your own house.'

She wished with all her heart that they hadn't invited Mark. He was too young, too wild and too thoughtless. The Hennessys had invited him only out of courtesy, so that he should not feel left out of it. Colin was Gerald Hennessy's friend, not Mark. Mark was only just eleven.

'The Hennessys,' she went on, 'are very wealthy people and there are many beautiful things in their home that are easy to break, things they have brought back from all over the world.' (She didn't know for certain; she had never been in the Hennessy's home; but it seemed a reasonable supposition to make.) 'Do be careful, Mark. Please don't *run* from room to room. Walk! Lift your feet! Look where you're going. And for heaven's sake don't go to bed with your singlet on.'

Mark nodded absently but Colin gave the right sort of smile and the right kind of reply. (After all, it was expected of him.) 'I'll keep an eye on him, Mum.'

'I'm relying on you, Colin. He's to keep his hands clean and his hair tidy and he's *not* to belch after meals.'

'I'll flatten him if he does!'

'I'm sure it won't come to that! You are merely to remind him of his responsibility to behave. Mrs Hennessy will have enough to do without contending with an eleven-year-old savage in the house. With six children around for the whole week-end her hands will be full.'

'More than six,' said Colin, with a feeling of satisfaction that his mother failed to notice, 'ten, more like it. There are the neighbours, you know, and they've so far to come that they'll be staying, too.'

'I'm not worried about the neighbours. Any neighbours the Hennessys might have will *know* how to behave. They're *used* to that sort of living! And there's one thing I'm bound to ask of you, Colin. Be nice to Jan. Don't be rude to her.'

'Huh,' said Colin, for there were areas of hostility even in the life of a well-mannered boy.

'Colin!' said Mrs Kerr sharply.

'All right, all right. But what did they want to go and ask her for?'

Janet sat disconsolately in front of her dressing-table mirror staring at herself. Her week-end bag was packed and waiting on the bed; in the next room was Bruce warbling for joy like a Swiss yodeller, and her mother was yelling from the back of the house, 'Come on, you two, or the car will be here before you've had your lunch!'

Honest to goodness, Janet knew that lots of girls got all the pleasure in the world out of looking at themselves in the mirror. Even some downright ugly girls (of limited powers of observation) could regard their own reflections with gratitude and admiration. But Janet was either too frank or too critical or too easily depressed. Whenever she felt miserable and wanted to feel worse, she usually made her way to her room and shut the door and said, 'Mirror, Mirror on the Wall; who's the crummiest of them all? Tell me, and I'll put a brick through you!'

Janet never looked at herself critically when she was happy, of course. She didn't think about it then. If she had, she might have discovered that a snub nose, freckles,

high cheek bones, a broad brow and an impish disposition
had a very real charm all of their own. But Janet wasn't
even faintly vain, so she would probably remain unaware
of herself until some nice young fellow in a few years' time
made the discovery for her.

At the present moment, the trouble was that she didn't
really *want* to go to Coonabibba. It might be fun to fly
300 miles there and back in the aeroplane – if she managed
not to be air-sick – and to stay for three days on a famous
sheep station, but it all came back to Gerald Hennessy,
didn't it? And how could she cut Gerald Hennessy out of
it? It was his home. It was his week-end. It was his party.

She had never been greatly impressed by Gerald Hennessy. There seemed to be something phoney about him,
though it wasn't anything she could really name with fair-
ness. He was just too clever, too good looking, too free
with his money and too well dressed.

None of it was Gerald's fault, he couldn't help being
born intelligent and generous and handsome, nor was he
to be blamed for all that the accident of his circumstances
had blessed him with. It was not his fault that his father
had inherited the Crown leasehold of 800 square miles of
semi-desert grasslands and salt bush west of the River
Darling, ideally suited to the growth of fine merino wool.
But in a way Janet did hold these things against him (and
his father as well), even though Bruce, her brother, was
one of Gerald's best friends.

She didn't think it was right that people should have
everything so easy when her own father was twice the man
Mr Hennessy would ever be, yet was always struggling to
pay the bills. Just as Bruce – so like his father – would one
day have to struggle to pay his bills, while Gerald would
lord it over his inherited kingdom out in the glowing west
where the sun set.

She didn't believe for a moment that it was Gerald himself who had thought of inviting her to his fourteenth birthday party. He would have invited Carol Bancroft – Carol was his type. Carol might not have a wealthy family behind her, but she had poise and polish and maturity way ahead of her thirteen years. By contrast and in her company, Janet often felt like something that the cat had dragged in. It was not that she was jealous – of Gerald or of Carol – but something about them both made her mad.

She believed her own invitation was a sympathy invitation from Gerald's mother, perhaps based on the mistaken hope that Janet would be good company for Carol, or because she was Bruce Martin's twin sister. (People spoke of *obligations* where twins were concerned.) It was not that Janet actually feared her week-end at Coonabibba; there were occasions when she felt very excited about it, when she thought of sheep and horses and desert sunrises, but she felt out of it, rather like a gatecrasher, as though she had not the slightest right to be going there.

Bruce burst in. 'Come on, Jan. Stir yourself. Mum's havin' hysterics. The lunch is spoiling, she says.'

The taxi tooted for Gerald at twelve-fifty and his aunt said, 'Bye-bye, darling. Happy birthday tomorrow.' Then she pecked him on the cheek and shut the door before he reached the front gate. He heard the door close and stopped for a moment in his stride. Yes, the door was certainly shut and she had gone back to her ancestral parlour where the blinds were drawn, back to her midday film on television, a drippy old film made in the year dot about a poor little rich girl who had everything in the world she wanted, absolutely everything, happiness and all. Of course she was terribly miserable about it. That was the point of the story. It didn't make sense to Gerald, or to anyone else probably, except to people like his aunt. She'd rushed back to it to shed another tear or two.

Gerald shrugged his shoulders (what did he care?) and smiled, not awkwardly, but with self-consciousness at the taxi driver. He knew the driver. Bert. Everybody called him Bert. What his other name was Gerald had no idea. Unless it was *Taxis*. That was how he was listed in the phone book.

'Hi,' said Gerald; but he knew that Bert expected more of him. He could see it from the look on the man's face, that twisted look, caused by more than the midday glare. 'Oh, *her*,' he said, 'don't take any notice of her. There's a film on.'

But Bert hadn't come down in the last shower. He knew. There was a woman like it in his own family. 'Does she ever wave good-bye, or is there always a film on?'

'Gosh,' said Gerald. 'I'm only going for three days.'

'That's not the point, kid.'

Gerald shrugged. 'Maybe not, but I don't care.' He didn't either. What was the use of caring? His aunt would never change. There was always a conversation something like this when he rode in Bert's taxi.

The man tossed him the key. 'Put your bag in the boot, kid.' Bert was like that. Independent. He was noted for it. No one took offence as a rule. Then Gerald slid on to the front seat beside him.

'Who next, kid?'

'Do you know the Bancrofts?'

'In Macquarie Street?'

Gerald nodded. 'Then the Kerrs at number fourteen Jacaranda Street and the Martins at twenty-three Waratah Street. O.K.?'

'Yep.' Bert moved off and squinted at the boy. 'Don't pick your friends from the toffee-noses, do you?'

Gerald shrugged again. Some things were difficult to answer. He wasn't nervous of Bert, not actually nervous, but usually in his company he found himself moving slightly to the defensive. Bert knew he was a Hennessy, of a long line of Hennessys. Bert himself was a working man – or called himself one – with no great love of the Squatting Class. Of course, no one called the Hennessys *squatters* any more, but *pastoralist* had the same sort of ring about it, the same aura of privilege and wealth that angered certain people. That Bert employed labour himself and owned six taxis didn't count. Not to Bert. Not when he was baiting Gerald. 'Does Dad approve of your friends, kid? Takin' them home to the baronial hall?'

'Of course.' (There had been questions; but Gerald had no intention of discussing them with Bert.)

'I'd have thought the toffs here on Phillip Street would have been more in your line.'

'You thought wrong, didn't you?'

'Yep,' said Bert, 'I did, didn't I? How come you don't go to one of them posh colleges in Sydney?'

'I don't know,' said Gerald, 'too far, I suppose.'

'The Richmonds send their kids and the Kingsfords send theirs and they're farther west than you are.'

'The Richmond boys and the Kingsfords only get home three times a year,' Gerald said. 'I like to get home once a month.'

'That figures,' said Bert, 'livin' in that old crow's nest I guess you'd want to get home once a month.'

'That's not fair! You'll apologize for that!'

Bert flashed a grin. 'I'm only pullin' your leg, kid. You're all right. You'll do. Any kid of a squatter who's in High School must be all right.'

Bert still wasn't saying the right things, not as far as

Gerald was concerned, but he wasn't keen for an argument. Gerald got flustered in arguments, particularly in
arguments with men who had faces like Bert, and Bert
knew it. It was a coarse face, the sort of face that came out
of the gutters of London a century and a half ago. 'There's
a breed,' Gerald's father had once said, 'that will wear that
face until the end of time. Coarseness. It's in them. Steer
clear of them, son.'

Why should Gerald think of that now?

The taxi tooted again. They had come to the Bancroft's
house in Macquarie Street and Carol was already moving
off the porch with her mother. Carol was carrying her own
bag and was wearing a flouncy floral frock, too old for her
years, but not too old for Carol. Girls, as a rule, didn't
interest Gerald over much, but everything about Carol
excited him – she was *good* to know – and he hurried from
the car to take the bag from her.

'Hullo, Carol,' he said. 'Hullo, Mrs Bancroft . . . so nice
of you to allow Carol to come.'

Mrs Bancroft didn't mind! Not where anything with
people like the Hennessys was concerned. 'She'll be in
good hands,' she simpered, 'and it'll be a marvellous ex-
perience for her. You've never been on a sheep station
before, have you, Carol?'

'No, Mother.'

They were not at all alike, mother and daughter, though
Mrs Bancroft had probably looked like Carol once. Carol
already had poise that her mother would never acquire.
Carol had a feeling for words, a tactfulness and a quality
of voice that in a very quiet way apologized for her
mother's manner, without actually humiliating her
mother. Of course, not everyone realized that; and Gerald
was not old enough to see it or to suspect it. The Mrs
Bancroft he knew and the mother that Carol knew were

two different people. Even the Carol that Gerald knew and the real Carol were two different people.

Bert tossed the key out again. Gerald caught it in his free hand and dropped Carol's bag into the luggage boot.

'Don't spoil her, Gerald,' Mrs Bancroft said, 'she's spoilt enough already, you know.'

Gerald smiled warmly.

'I know you'll both have a perfectly wonderful time. You do seem to go together so well.'

Gerald didn't mind hearing that either, but Bert grimaced and ran a finger round his collar, and Carol said, 'Good-bye, Mother, don't worry, and I'll keep a slice of birthday cake for you. . . . I suppose there is a cake, Gerald?'

'Gosh,' said Gerald, 'if there isn't I'll want to know why.'

In a few moments the car was moving again and Mrs Bancroft was left at the kerb, alone and faintly nervous. She was jealous of her daughter and of what her daughter might become, but she loved her in a frightened way just the same.

Carol sat beside Gerald and Bert said, 'So it's a birthday you're havin'?'

'That's right,' said Gerald.

'And you're takin' your schoolmates home for the celebration?'

'Yes.'

'Horse ridin' and tennis parties and barbecues and all?'

'I suppose so.'

'Very democratic,' said Bert, 'but six of you won't make a very big party.'

'There are others,' said Gerald, with renewed caution.

'Ah,' said Bert, 'mixin' 'em up, eh? The blue-bloods and the hoi polloi.'

'Oh for Pete's sake,' flared Gerald, 'what have I ever

done to you? What do you always want to be picking on me for?'

Bert grinned. 'I'm not pickin' on you, kid. I'm the sort of friend a kid like you needs. What do you say, miss?'

'I say you have a strange way of behaving like a friend.'

'Yep,' said Bert, 'put a silly question and get a silly answer. . . . Kerr's place, you said?'

'Yes.'

Bert tooted, but there wasn't any need. Mark was erupting from the house and Mrs Kerr was to be seen behind him with fingers clenched to her temples, a not uncommon attitude for her. She had problems, poor woman, and all of them began with Mark. Bert said, 'Here comes the holy terror.' And Mrs Kerr screeched, 'Mark! Wait for Colin.' And Colin, in his best suit, endeavouring without success to give the impression that Mark belonged to someone else, walked with dignity to the gate with a book in one hand and a suitcase in the other.

'Hi,' he said to Gerald and Carol, but wasn't heard. It was Mark's moment – not Colin's – Mark scrambling into the back seat declaring, 'Coonabibba, here we come!'

'Take them feet off the seat,' barked Bert, 'or you'll be goin' nowhere, not even to the air-strip.'

Colin at last caught Gerald's eye and wiggled his suitcase. 'What can I do with this?'

The key came out to Colin, then he turned and waved to his mother. 'Good-bye!'

'So long, Mum,' shrilled Mark.

'Good-bye,' she called, and they drove away.

She stood as though stunned, for a surprising length of time, then went back inside and put the kettle on for a cup of tea.

At 23 Waratah Street, where the Martins lived, it was

different again. There Bert tooted twice and would have tooted a third time if Bruce had not appeared at the door to shout, 'Coming! Won't be a tick. Jan's got something in her eye.'

Janet was crying. She didn't want to go. This she had decided suddenly, but refused to say why. 'I don't want to go, that's all.'

It was Carol. Carol was a lady and Janet was a crumb. Janet didn't want to look like something that the cat had dragged in for three whole days.

Funny; much the same sort of face on Bruce looked just right; on her it was a calamity. But she had not allowed her face to upset her life before. It had made her miserable often enough but never to the point that it had involved other people.

'But *why?*' cried her mother. 'You must have a reason. People don't get into a state like yours without a reason. You've been so excited about it.'

'I haven't. I don't want to go. I don't want to go.'

'Are you frightened of the aeroplane or something?' She had covered every other possibility. How could a mother guess the real reason? She thought Janet was beautiful!

'No, no,' said Janet.

'Have you had a dream or anything?' (Janet's dreams interested Mrs Martin; she was sure the child was psychic.) 'A premonition of danger or anything?'

'No, no, no.'

'Well what *has* it to do with?'

'It doesn't matter.'

'It does matter.'

'I just don't want to go.' With tight lips and teeth showing.

'But you will, you know,' roared Bruce, 'by crikey you will.'

'I'd like to see you make me!'

'Janet,' said her mother fiercely, 'an invitation has been issued, you have accepted it and you will honour it. You are to go to the bathroom, you are to wash your face, and you are to come at once to the door.'

'No.'

'Janet, I order you!'

That was final in the Martin household; it always had been; so Janet went, sobbing, and Bruce said to his mother, 'For crying out loud, what's wrong with her?'

'It's her age.' That was the desperate sort of generalization that covered everything when nothing else fitted.

'I don't know what her age has got to do with it. She's the same age as me. What's so special about it?'

'You wouldn't understand.'

'You can say that again.'

'She's a girl; not a boy. Neither child nor woman.'

'And what does that make me?'

'Oh, I don't know, I don't know. I'm not worried about you. Go on down to the car and tell them she's coming. *Take* the luggage! Don't leave it for me to carry. Janet's too.'

Bruce groaned, mumbled something under his breath, then snatched at the bags and stalked out.

Mrs Martin went to the bathroom and found Janet sobbing into the washbasin. 'What is it, darling?' she said. 'Come on. Tell me.'

'I can't. You'd be angry. Or you'd laugh.'

'Mothers don't laugh at daughters. They were girls themselves once, you know.'

'I can't tell you, Mummy. I can't.'

'Very well. Wash that face and dry it. Hurry on. You're

behaving badly. You're delaying other people.'

'Oh, Mummy,' said Janet.

'It's the aeroplane, isn't it, or you have had a dream?'

'*No.*'

Janet washed her face and took the towel from her mother's hand and somehow managed to stifle her sobbing, to hold it down. It wasn't easy, because everything had got away from her; problems seemed so much bigger than they had been before.

'Are you composed?'

She wasn't, but she nodded. 'Very well; we'll discuss this at a later date. Come along.'

After the car had gone, the woman turned quickly indoors and rang her husband. 'Len,' she said, 'I'm worried. I've had a terrible scene with Janet. I'm convinced she's been dreaming again.'

He sighed, just a little.

'I'm sure she's had a premonition. Probably about the aeroplane.'

'Look here,' he said, 'what if she has? What does it prove? She's gone, hasn't she?'

'Yes.'

'Well, for heaven's sake stop worrying.'

Later, she was to reproach him for that.

2. Carol

Carol was apparently full of concern for Jan's swollen eyes and Jan was furious about it. (She was never known as Janet except at home.) 'No, no, no,' she protested. 'It's all right now. Honest it is. It was only an insect. It's gone now.'

'But it must have hurt so.'

'It hurt all right,' said Bruce. 'You should have heard her.'

'But it's in both eyes,' persisted Carol, 'not one.'

'I cried,' said Jan desperately. She could take anybody's sympathy but Carol Bancroft's. 'You know what it's like when something's in your eye.'

Carol did know, that was the point, and she didn't think it was something to cry about with both eyes, not when you were thirteen years old, but it was so difficult to talk to Jan about anything.

'Forget it,' Jan said. 'Please. I was a bit of a baby but I couldn't help it.'

Carol wasn't really being nasty but she could see that Jan thought she was. It was a shame that Jan was in the crowd. She would probably end up spoiling the week-end for everybody. That twins could be so unlike one another was a mystery. Bruce was good fun. Admittedly, he wasn't like Gerald – Gerald was rather special – but Bruce was good company just the same and sometimes the life and

21

soul of the party. When people were having fun they never counted Bruce out.

Bert chipped in. He knew something was up and he didn't want a howling match – or a stand-up fight – in his taxi. 'I wouldn't say you were bein' a baby about it, miss. I have trouble with me left eye with things gettin' in it, and the other one always starts up in sympathy. Tears pourin' down me cheeks. Embarrassin', I can tell you.'

'Huh,' sniffed Mark, to whom all tears, except his own, were a mark of weakness. 'Wouldn't catch me cryin' just for somethin' in me eye.'

'You're usually too busy howling, anyway,' said Colin, 'to take time off for that.'

'I am not,' shouted Mark.

'Sit still,' said Bert, 'and keep your voice down. I can't stand shriekin' kids. If you want to ride in a taxi with grown-ups behave like one.'

'Grown-ups?' howled Mark, 'What grown-ups?'

'All right,' barked Bert. 'Shriek again and out! One more time, that's all!'

Mark grumbled and felt self-conscious and shrank into his corner, then realized that Carol had turned her head and was looking at him sternly. Just like a bloomin' school-teacher. It was going to be a great week-end if a fella couldn't open his mouth. Carol was thinking much the same sort of thing, though from a different angle. She was thinking that Colin Kerr was all right in a quiet sort of way, but that the one thing wrong with him was his brother. Mark was a pest. Between the two of them – Mark and Jan – the week-end at Coonabibba had a shadow over it even before it started. She couldn't work out why the Hennessys had asked either of them. They were both mis-fits. There wasn't much to pick between the two of them.

'What's your book, Colin?' said Bruce, to change the subject.

'Eh?'

'Your book?'

'Oh. *Oliver Twist.*'

'Crikey. You haven't brought your school-work with you, have you?'

'Not exactly. I didn't think it'd hurt to read it, though. We've got to read it sometime, haven't we?'

'Gee. You're keen.'

'Well, Mr Crampton did say it, didn't he? That if he gave us the time off to get away early we had to make it up.'

'He was only *joking*,' said Gerald. 'He didn't mean it. He always lets me off half a day early when I'm going home. You won't have time to read, anyway, not with everything that Mother's got planned for us.'

'What?' said Mark with interest. 'What's planned?'

'All sorts of things. Even a friend for you.'

'Fair dinkum?'

'Lesley Harrington'll be there,' said Gerald.

'Who's he?'

'She lives at Vernon – that's the next property.'

'A girl!' wailed Mark.

'Well, don't go reckoning on sticking in my pocket for the week-end,' growled Colin. 'You can forget that idea.'

Mark was about to shriek again but Bert's peaked cap caught his eye and Gerald said, 'Lesley's brother will be there, but he's younger, of course.'

'How much younger?'

'Six.'

'Swipe me,' moaned Mark and sank back in his corner, pouting.

Colin said, 'Who else will be there?'

'A crowd,' said Gerald, 'a really good crowd. Mother

knows how to do these things, you know. There'll be a
few older ones – about thirty all told, I reckon. They're
coming from miles around. From as far as the Manning's,
200 miles up-country.'

'Gee,' said Bruce, 'I didn't know that. Why didn't you
tell a fellow?'

'Beaut,' said Colin with a sideways glance at Jan. He
had had a sneaking suspicion that his fate was to have
been linked with hers for the week-end, but with the odds
lengthening at this rate there was a chance that it wouldn't
be. 'Oh, beaut,' he said. 'Yeah, you could have told us,
Gerald.'

'And spoil half your fun? No fear. The Hennessys know
how to run a party. It's a week-end of surprises.' Gerald
grinned. 'Maybe surprises for me, too. I don't know.
Mother just loves dropping things on you without warning.'

Bert looked sour as Gerald went on talking. 'Then on
Sunday we're going out to Silver Creek. It's a drive of
ninety miles in the old blitz buggy. A real thrill.'

'Where the opals come from?'

'That's right. Be able to pick yourselves up a few chips.'

'Real opals?' said Jan, shaking herself out of her misery
for the first time.

'Real opals,' said Gerald, and gave Carol a nudge that
might have meant that more surprises were in store, that
not only chips were to be found. That was what she took
the nudge to mean, anyway. An opal on a pendant or an
opal on a ring was a nice kind of thought.

'Really got it organized, kid,' said Bert, 'haven't you?'

'I suppose so. Why not?'

'I'm all for it,' said Bert, 'I'm not criticizin'. All depends
though, doesn't it?'

'On what?'

'On the aeroplane turnin' up?'

'Golly,' said Bruce, 'won't it? It'll turn up, won't it, Gerald?'

'It'll be there,' said Gerald. 'Probably there by now.'

'How are you goin' to fit all this lot in?' said Bert, for the devil of it. 'It's not a bloomin' air liner.'

'They'll fit.'

Mark sat up and took notice. If there wasn't room for everybody he knew who'd get left behind!

'Kids,' sniffed Bert, 'flyin' here and there in aeroplanes just like they were pushbikes. In my time we walked or stayed home. Stayed home mostly. Kids these days get it easy. Unless they're like *them*, of course!' And jerked his thumb at Shanty Town on the north shore flats of the lake. 'Yeh, unless you're an abo kid, I guess.'

'Come off it, Bert,' said Gerald. And Gerald really meant it. With sudden anger. Shanty Town made him sick. He always turned his head away when he passed. 'And what have you ever done for the aborigines, anyway, except take their money off them?'

'You hold your tongue! I give 'em somethin' for their money. I never robbed a man in me life, black or white. I give 'em a ride and treat 'em square. It's more than your mob's ever done for 'em.'

That wasn't fair of Bert; he was a man nearly fifty years of age and he should have known better. The boy might have been rude, but there was more to it than simple anger. Much more. Sensitive things that belonged to the good heart of a boy that men like Bert had forgotten or had never felt or had never known.

The car fell silent.

And Carol blushed. It was stupid of her. The burning flush came up and she could not suppress it. It burned until her eyes smarted.

They saw it; they couldn't help but see it. But they didn't understand. They thought she felt for Gerald. (Crumbs, thought Jan, she's human.) They knew nothing of the skeleton in the Bancroft's cupboard, the great-grandmother in the family tree.

'She's beautiful,' her mother had whispered on the day that Carol had been born. 'She's white.'

Silly woman. (As if Carol could have been anything else.) She should never have told the girl.

3. Colin

They were not sorry to reach the air-strip. Bert was an old sourpuss. Of course, he was renowned for it; always picking on kids; always moaning about something. He had spoilt everything for the time being, and now they knew things wouldn't start looking up until they got rid of him.

'Old crumb he is,' mumbled Mark under his breath, 'maybe he's got a bellyache or somethin'.' Or perhaps it was the sort of day when all grown-ups had bellyaches. His mum had been the same: nag, nag, nag. And Mrs Martin had come down the path bashing Jan's ear, hardly stopping for breath. Maybe Jan had been crying for that, rather than for what she'd got in her eye. Mark liked Jan. She didn't have tickets on herself. Not like that other fussy-britches, that Carol, with the long-nosed glare and the hoity-toity ways. She even wore *lip-stick* . . . and sun-glasses like birds' wings. Enough to give a fella the creeps.

The *Egret* was there all right. They knew it was there even before they arrived (which was one in the eye for old Bert) because they saw the man from the oil depot driving his utility truck away. Not that he waved when he passed; not that he smiled or anything. Didn't even nod at Bert. Just roared past in a cloud of dust going about fifty miles an hour when thirty would have been enough. That was something else for Bert to snarl about, because his car was black and polished like a mirror, and the air was too still to clear the dust from the track. He nosed into a fog of it and they had to wind up the windows. It had been a dry summer, a hard summer for dust in the west, with frequent high winds and stifling calms. It was just about due to break, surely. The plains were burnt to a crisp, grass was brown or earth bare even along the river banks, and in the marshes black mud had set like crazed concrete and turned to grey. Only the trees were green, though their foliage was dusty and dirty. It wasn't a real drought, but it could become one if rain held off for much longer.

The car run out on to the strip, into clearer air, and the *Egret* came into view, a small, high-winged monoplane with a radial engine and a closed cabin. She had a yellow fuselage, white rudder and black wings and tailplane. The colours were an insult to the eye, deliberately so. The plane was painted, not to merge into the western land-scape, but to be distinct from it, to be clearly visible on the ground in the event of mishap or forced landing. Not that the *Egret* made a habit of that sort of thing. It was a particularly good little aeroplane, reliable and robust, a lucky little aeroplane with a history entirely free of incidents and accidents.

'There she is,' said Gerald needlessly.

She was a great sight. She spelt adventure, and escape from Bert and his taxi. For once, Bert knew that he had gone too far, but the art of making an apology was not his strength. He did try to smooth things over but it didn't work out. Gerald paid the fare and Bert said, 'You'll be back about eight o'clock Monday morning, I suppose?'

'I expect so.'

'O.K. I'll be waiting for you.'

'You can wait if you like, but not for me. I'd rather walk.'

By then the others were out, the boys were heaving the luggage from the boot, and the pilot of the aeroplane had

wandered over from the shade of the wing for a chat. Or
at least that appeared to have been his intention until he
heard the tone of Gerald's voice. Then he turned away.

Bert had nothing more to say. He pocketed the fare and
drove off with a brow as black as thunder, leaving his
passengers grouped together, like people marooned on a
railway platform between trains. It was a strange sensation. Momentarily, they felt lost. Every one was out of
sorts, even the pilot. One look at his face was enough to
tell them that.

'Ready?' he said, as though he didn't care one way or
the other.

'Yes,' said Gerald, 'but that taxi driver!'

'What's up with him?'

'It's what he *said*.'

Jim Butler saw that as an invitation to pursue the topic,
but he couldn't be bothered; he'd had troubles enough of
his own with the character from the oil depot. Not that it
had come to words, but there had been an undercurrent
of irritability, a lack of patience and of common courtesy.
Perhaps the fault had been Jim's. He was honest enough
to admit that. He didn't feel his usual self. It was one of
those days. And now a plane-load of children to cap it off.
They'd better behave!

'Have you all flown before?' he said. And something in
his voice warned them that here was yet another grown-up
of uncertain humour. Though he looked a nice enough
man, rather like somebody's fond father, they knew he
wasn't. Gerald had told them that he was a drifter, an
adventurer who had turned his hand to a dozen jobs in
as many countries round the world.

Colin said, indicating Mark, 'We haven't been up before.'

Jim grunted. 'But the rest of you have?'

It appeared that they had, if nods meant anything.

'Any of you get air-sick?'

Jan looked awkward. 'Sometimes,' she said.

'Yeh,' agreed Bruce. 'All times, she means.'

'Air-sick?' squealed Mark. 'How can air make you sick?'

'The aeroplane, son,' said Jim, taking the lad's measure. Mischief written all over him. Give him an inch and he'd take a mile. Jim marked him down mentally as a character to be dealt with severely. 'It's the aeroplane, son, not the air. Just as it's the ship, not the sea . . . Anyway, we'll soon find out. And so will you. What's your name?'

'Mark.'

'Sorry,' said Gerald, 'I should have introduced you, but that Bert's got me all stewed up. No matter what he says he's always having a shot at you.'

Jim shrugged. 'I'll pick them up as we go along and then I'll remember them. You, lassie?'

'Jan Martin.'

'I think you'd better sit up front with me, Jan. If you've got something to watch maybe you'll feel less like being sick.' This was a disappointment for Gerald. That was *his* seat. Sometimes Jim let him fly! 'And there's one thing you're all to remember,' Jim went on. 'Stay put. She's no air liner; if you start moving round you'll upset the trim; and I want a nice, steady flight. No excitement, no horse-play. You'll be in the air for three hours. I want three hours of good behaviour. And you – Mark – any nonsense and I'll chuck you over the side.'

'Crikey,' wailed Mark, 'what have I done, mister?'

'Nothing,' said Jim, 'and that's the way I want it. And call me Jim. No frills. Plain Jim.'

Jan didn't know about that. She doubted whether she could call a man old enough to be her father by his Christian name, and oddly enough she caught Colin's eye.

Colin's expression seemed to suggest the same doubts. Then Carol said, 'I've brought some barley sugar, Jim. Perhaps that'll help the ones who might feel sick.'

'Just the thing. Hand it round. You're – ?'

'Carol.'

'Very thoughtful of you, Carol. All right, all aboard. See to the luggage, will you, Gerald, and see if you can do it without my having to restack it!'

Jim took the *Egret* to the end of the strip, Jan beside him in the right-hand seat, tense and erect, her piece of barley sugar already crushed between her teeth, her pulse already quickening, her safety belt, if anything, too tightly drawn.

Was this really why she had not wanted to go? Was it the fear of physical wretchedness, this awful sickness that was at the bottom of it, rather than Gerald or Carol or looking like something that the cat had dragged in? Perhaps it was the aeroplane all the time. Perhaps her mother was right. Perhaps everything else was just an excuse to conceal the *real* fear.

The lake was scarcely a hundred yards away. Birds disturbed from the shore-line reeds scattered across the open water in a flurry of beating wings – a soundless flurry. They could hear nothing but the rumble and crack of the *Egret*. She had a healthy engine, with a snarl in the exhaust. It was an engine like a predator in its prime, sound in wind and limb, vocal, full of fight.

Jim throttled back and stood cross-wind – not that there was any surface wind to speak of – and checked his cockpit. The altimeter, he noticed with surprise, required an adjustment of several hundred feet: that meant the barometer was falling. A weather report would be useful, but he couldn't get one here, not without the long-range trans-

mitter that the *Egret* lacked. Wealthy people were sometimes mean in curious ways. Hennessy had said, 'Too
expensive. No call for it.' It was a statement that Jim had
felt like rubbishing.

He throttled fully back and shouted, 'Who heard the
midday news? Anyone?'

'I did,' Colin yelled from behind.

'What'd they say about the weather?'

'Continuing hot, I think.'

'Lot of drongos,' said Jim, 'barometer's falling like a
brick.'

He advanced the throttle, turned the aircraft a few
degrees, then locked the brakes again. That brought the
sky in the south and the west into view. He was right:
cirrus was coming in at about 15,000 feet. The blue was
whitening. 'See that,' he yelled, 'weather's coming! I hope
you've packed your gum boots.'

'No,' said Jan, wide-eyed.

Jim turned a keen eye on her and smiled reassuringly.
'Just my joke, lass. O.K. everybody. *Take off!*'

It was as sudden as that. Colin had expected something
more of a preamble, perhaps hoped for it, a pause of sus-
pense or anticipation, a bristling of feathers perhaps. Instead, the *Egret* swung on to the strip, roared mightily,
and lumbered off dragging her tail along the ground like
a log of wood, jolting and jarring and vibrating, as though
determined to shake Colin's teeth from his head. Colin
sat on the floor, squashed up among shoes and legs, his
best suit already soiled with dust. There were four seats
at the back but Colin made the fifth and – so often the
perfect gentleman – had insisted upon his own discomfort,
though for weeks he had longed to watch the take-off, to
treasure the first golden moment of flight.

Oh, the movements down there on the floor were most

peculiar; the change from rough to smooth, the hard and shattering assault of sound. Dust puffed over him, his back bent in the middle, his stomach dropped a foot until he was sure he was sitting on it. He felt giddy, bloodless, and suddenly sick, and he had to swallow very, very firmly, and close his eyes tightly. The *Egret* might have been a hundred feet up or a hundred feet underground. He didn't know and he didn't care.

In a moment he left a hand on his shoulder and looked up, panting. It was Gerald. His lips seemed to be framing the words, 'Are you all right?'

Colin didn't know whether he was all right or not. It was too soon to say. Oh, it was an awful, awful feeling. Gerald bent lower. His face came very close and looked strained. 'Take my seat!'

Gerald started struggling out of his seat, trying not to stand on Colin. There was so little room and so much noise, and the aircraft was climbing so steeply that Colin was scared to move, almost too scared to breathe. He was going to be *sick*.

He groaned for air. He felt terrible, ashamed, weak, sore. And he couldn't stop. 'I'm sorry,' he moaned, but no one heard him. They couldn't hear him and didn't want to, anyway.

If he had been sick in any other way it would have been different. If he had broken a leg or caught a fever it would have been quite another thing. Their thoughts then would not have been for themselves. Even the shame they felt now was for themselves; that they *knew* him.

All Gerald could do was to fall back in his seat and turn his head away, dismayed and angry, sorry that he had ever asked the Kerrs, either of them, Colin or his pest of a brother. That was what his eyes said to Carol: 'Who would have guessed it?'

Even Mark was aghast. He couldn't believe that this had happened to Colin – Colin, the brother who took everything so seriously, who always did the right thing. He looked like one of those horrible men who got drunk and sat in gutters. Mark just didn't understand. Colin had looked forward to it all so much, he'd been so excited about it.

4. Jim

Jan sat perfectly still. She was sweating like a statue of ice thawing in a warm room. Oh, she wished Jim wouldn't climb so steeply. Jim soared the plane like a kite, he seemed to hang the *Egret* from her propeller blades as one might hang a sheet to a high line from a single peg.

The earth beneath, the lake, the plains, seemed to lean back and slide over the edge of the world. The *Egret* could climb, really climb; her makers had intended that she should. They had sold more of her kind to the armies of the world than they had sold to people like the Hennessys. The *Egret* in army parlance had another name, a name that expressed her toughness, her usefulness, her lust for work.

Jim took her up and up and the earth flattened into formlessness, heat-hazed, became a vast raft of drab reds and yellows and purples, that continued to tilt, continued to slide over the edge of the world. The sky ahead was streaked with wind, with long streamers of cloud fragmented like foam on a beach.

Jan held on, fighting against herself, clutching the stout paper bag that Jim had given her, eyes closed now against the glare, nostrils dilated, nerves plucking at her knees and thighs, trembling inside, still unaware of Colin's plight, cut off from it by the engine's roar and her tense concern for the delicate balance of her own stomach. But Jim was not unaware of it; he smelt it first, threw a hand to his head in irritation, and glanced back. He saw four children sitting erect with pained expressions, as though the unfortunate wretch at their feet was an object of disgust, not of sympathy. Jim waved an angry arm at Gerald. 'Do something,' that arm said. 'Don't sit there.' But Gerald looked back in silent appeal and raised his open hands, helplessly. What *could* be done? It was too late.

'Clean him up!' bellowed Jim.

Gerald couldn't hear, but Jan did. She opened her eyes and slightly, carefully, turned her head and looked at Jim, then saw the command in his expression suddenly switch on to her. 'Look to the front,' he bellowed and pointed ahead. Jan didn't see what had happened behind her, but in that instant she knew, and immediately was ill herself. Her body convulsed; sobbing, she buried her face in the bag.

'For Pete's sake,' wailed Jim. '*Kids!*'

He throttled back and steadied on 120 knots at about 4,000 feet. He had wanted to go higher, he had wanted to find tail winds, but not with sick children all over the place!

'Gerald,' he screamed, 'Do something with that boy.' Then he glanced again at Jan. She was well away, poor kid, but at least she was orderly, at least she was prepared. The lad, by the look of it, had been caught napping. *Two* of them at the same time! And there were almost three hours in the air still ahead of them. Jim felt it wasn't his day.

'You do it,' Gerald screamed at Mark. 'He's your brother.'

'Do what?' cried Mark. Colin was the colour of pasteboard, like someone at death's door; he was limp, like someone with broken bones. There were even tears on his cheeks. It was too much. And Mark wasn't feeling over-

well himself. He was only eleven, after all. Eleven only
month ago. He still felt as though he was only ten. Or
maybe nine. The longer he thought about it, the younger
he felt. He didn't want to have to touch Colin. He wanted
to look at the view. He'd never been up in an aeroplane
before!

'Take his suit off,' Gerald screamed. 'I'm blowed if I'm
going to do it. Then chuck it out the window or something. Get rid of the horrible thing.'

'Eh?'

'Oh! Wash your ears out!'

'I can't hear,' cried Mark. 'I don't know what you're
saying.'

'It'd be better to chuck *them* out, not their clothes!'
Bruce howled in Gerald's ear.

'What?'

'Chuck out Colin, and Jan too. Out of the window. It'll
be easier!'

Gerald didn't think it was funny.

'Oh, shut up!'

It was all right for Bruce. He was stuck in the back out
of harm's way. He didn't have to do anything. He couldn't
unless Gerald moved first.

Carol took hold of Gerald's arm and squeezed it. She
didn't say anything but she didn't need to. Gerald knew
what she meant. She was asking him to do it. But he
couldn't. Gerald hated dirt, hated mess, hated smells. It
was an abhorrence that was stronger than loyalties, stronger than friendship. Gerald wasn't neat and tidy be
he was a wealthy man's son, but was simpl
was Gerald. He had no tie with this cr
The Colin he knew he admired f
quietness, his cleanliness:
the same things. And J

hose Bruce as a friend. They were complete opposites. Perhaps Bruce was the foil.

Bruce yelled: 'Come on, Gerald. Fair crack of the whip.'

And Carol still squeezed his arm, though he tried to pretend that her hand was not there.

Colin struggled to move away from them towards the door, away from their legs and feet, away from the faces that he had looked to in vain. But there was nowhere to go. It wasn't like a ship or a house. There wasn't a bunk he could go to, or a cabin, or a bathroom. There wasn't anywhere private. They were all so close together. He couldn't get out of their sight. He couldn't retreat from them to clean himself up, to compose himself, for in truth he offended himself even more than he offended them. He was deeply hurt. Surely friends and brothers couldn't hate a fellow just because he was sick? He had never looked for help before to find the need shunned. There was love in his home. He had even thought there was love in Mark. There was the pilot, raving and shouting soundlessly; there were his friends frozen.

These were not ordered thoughts, or feelings that came to him clearly and distinctly one after the other in a logical way; they were all part of his overall hurt and resentment.

He tried to get his coat off by himself, but the effort made him sick again and they didn't even hand him a paper bag or a glass of water. He knew there was water in a canvas bag. He knew there was a plastic beaker. It was like something imagined in the middle of the night, when a fellow had gone to bed excited, and slept in fits and starts between bad dreams. It was then, only then, his friends edged towards him almost with loathing, with like Gerald turned away, a grey face that scarcely looked

t, distastefully turned it inside out,

rolled it up and pushed it away with his foot. Then he tried to take his trousers, but Colin wouldn't let him. He struck weakly at Gerald with his clenched fist and made himself sick again.

They looked at each other as they had never looked at each other before, drawing farther apart, shrinking from each other, almost hating each other: Gerald, for what Colin had made him do: Colin, for what Gerald had done too late. Then Colin couldn't sit up any more and Gerald with something like finality secured his seat belt again. Colin sagged at last on to his side, half twisted, half lying down, panting for breath, and almost at once fell asleep. It was the one escape that he could take, his only escape, and he had not imagined that it was there.

Jim could see what was going on, but was too impatient, too frustrated, to work out the reasons for it. All he could feel was an intense annoyance, an intense disappointment in the *quality* of the children. He was surprised, perhaps a bit shocked. Like Bert, he too had forgotten what it was like to be a boy – and he had forgotten something else, for he had long outgrown it. He had forgotten that the children were in the air. They were not themselves; part of them was left behind on the ground, far below, and they would not find it again until they returned to the ground; the finer edge, the sharper edge of feeling and common sense, even of simpler processes of thought. Jim had forgotten what it was like to be imprisoned in a vibrating box of sound high above the earth; he had forgotten the quiet insistence of the man who had taught him how to fly years ago, the repeating of things over and over again, the struggle to think, the struggle to work out the right heading to steer, the difficulty of obeying or carrying out efficiently the simplest order or duty. Jim had forgotten that even an intelligent and fully-grown man could behave like a perfect fool in the air until he became accustomed to it. It was one of those mysteries of the human mind and the human body. Man was born with two legs to walk on the ground, not with wings to fly.

Jan was asleep now beside him, lolling in her seat limply; all strength drained from her; held there by the harness buckled across her lap; just as well she hadn't followed his example and released her harness after take-off, or she would have fallen out. She was terribly pale and her hair hung over her forehead in strands. Jim decided, then, to go higher, to look for the tail-winds, if they were to be found.

He knew that at his present height he was in a freshening southerly stream. The aircraft was drifting to starboard, into the north, and he had had to alter course considerably to correct it. He didn't want to prolong the flight a minute longer than necessary. Two kids sick already; there might be more to come! That sort of thing, once started, was like measles. It was catching!

And he wanted to get to Coonabibba before the rain. Coonabibba was dry and dusty. There was a cushion of dust on the surface, soft underfoot like a deep-pile rug. Sheep would have been dying at Coonabibba if grass had been their mainstay, but succulent saltbush was the wealth of Coonabibba and it continued to thrive months after the last blade of grass had withered into the ground.

Rain would turn Coonabibba into a sea of red mud inches deep like a sea of treacle, that would pluck a man's shoes from his feet and stop a motor-car and pose a problem for an aircraft touching down. Jim had never seen it happen; he had seen Coonabibba only as a plain of dust stirring in the breezes, but Gerald's father had described it and on that point, on what rain meant to Coonabibba when it came without warning, he couldn't be wrong.

But was it rain in the sky or wind? Was it wind rushing north to fill the depression up Queensland way? High-level wind was no problem. Surface wind was dangerous. Surface wind meant dust and Jim had already had enough of dust for his liking. Trying to find Coonabibba homestead in a dust storm was like looking for a needle in a haystack.

He went up to 6,000 feet and then to 7,000, but the wind was still on his beam, still blowing from the south, drifting him to starboard. Jim needed no instruments to measure the wind, no computations by a navigator; his experienced eye judged the drift against purple smudges on the ground, against lonely roads, apparently endlessly straight, against the faint lines of trees that marked dried-up water-courses. To the inexperienced eye, the land beneath was featureless. To Jim it was a map, rich in detail, still clearly defining his track towards Coonabibba, but there were no tailwinds to be found, not at any height that he could reach without oxygen for his ailing passengers. The movement of the air was a massive movement from south to north; it bore all the marks of a major change in the pattern of the weather. He might reach Coonabibba before it broke, before it turned to blinding dust or rain, but the children were in for a rough weekend. There'd be no tennis or horse-riding or long drives in the blitz buggy. There would be a house full of people with nothing to do!

Jim glanced back again to check on the children. That was all he did; twisted his body and turned his head; but a pain as though a bullet had hit him wrenched through his chest.

His face registered astonishment more than pain; astonishment, not because he failed to understand, but because he did understand.

There was a motionless instant in time. In that instant he lived out the rest of his life.

His startled mind cried a question that he addressed to God. It was not a prayer, because he didn't have time for that, or the inclination. His mind cried silently: *'Why me? Why now? I'm only forty-four.'*

And so he died, astonished.

5. Gerald

Carol was watching him. She had seen him turn his head and her eyes had gone to his face. But his head and shoulders were against the light, shadowed against the glare, so that at first she did not see him in detail.

Carol liked the look of Jim. She hoped that the man she married some day would have a jaw like his, clean and square, manly but kind. She wondered in that instant whether Gerald would make a man like Jim. His hair was much the same colour, even the shape of his head was similar. But Gerald would grow taller than Jim, and probably leaner. Already he was tall for his age. Probably that was why he wore his clothes so well, good clothes of the right size – not short in the legs or tight under the arms liks Bruce's.

It was interesting, wondering what sort of man each boy in this aeroplane would become. The boy and the man, the same person, but so different. A snub-nosed boy like Bruce, full of fun, could become a man with wrinkles of worry and bitterness and blotchy skin, grey-haired or bald, needing a shave. She preferred fair men; dark men by the end of the day had shadows on their faces, blue or black shadows, almost like stains.

Something was wrong. Or was she imagining it? Jim's head was still turned towards her but his body seemed to be falling to one side towards Jan. It was some cruel, ridiculous trick of the light.

Suddenly, she grabbed at Gerald. In the same instant Bruce's hand came down like a hammer on Gerald's shoulder, and the aeroplane had dropped a wing and everything in it seemed to be sliding unnaturally to one side. The *Egret* was turning, but not as it should. The controls were crossed; it was skidding.

Mark screamed something. It was not a word, it was a boy's fear of the unknown and Gerald heard it faintly. He knew it came from someone else, but it seemed to express his own uncomprehending alarm.

'*Jim,*' he howled at the limit of his voice, lurching forward against his harness, throwing out an arm. He had never produced a louder sound nor one that had had less effect. It was impossible to converse in the *Egret* except by mouth to ear.

'Jim!' But Gerald wasn't addressing him any longer, not as a particular person or as a pilot of the *Egret*. He was crying the name as he might cry into a great silence or a black night, as he might cry as he fell from a cliff-top or into an animal trap, helplessly, wildly, in panic.

Jim had slipped now into an extraordinary attitude, right away from the controls, his head against Jan, his weight bearing on her in such a way that she, too, had slipped sideways until she could slip no farther, until her head and shoulders were hard against the side of the aircraft.

'What's wrong with him?' screamed Bruce. 'What's he doing?'

Gerald didn't know; not that he heard Bruce; it was simply that he was asking himself the same question, or trying to ask it, trying to frame the thought against the wishes of an almost commanding part of him that didn't want to know at all, that was afraid to know, that wanted to turn and run. In his mind he was doing that already.

He was running away from the situation as fast as he could.

'He's sick,' screamed Carol, shaking Gerald and pushing him. 'Go to him, Gerald! Help him!'

Gerald heard her, but he didn't want to move; he didn't want to admit that anything was wrong. Once that admission was made, all sorts of things that he scarcely dared think about would centre suddenly on him.

Jim couldn't be sick. He was a strong man. He had marked up thousands of hours in the air; he'd been a pilot of light aircraft for more than twenty years. He had flown in North America and the Antarctic and in Africa. Men like Jim didn't get sick in the air.

The aircraft was still slipping; it was beginning to lose height; beginning to go down in a wide and curious curve; and Jan was waking up, struggling under the weight that bore against her. Gerald saw her face twisting and straining, and knew that she was crying out, shouting; he could see that she could not dislodge Jim and that he seemed to be incapable of raising himself.

Gerald's mental block was still there, his panic was still there, and his fear of crossing the aircraft's centre of gravity was also there. He knew that if he moved forward the angle of dive must inevitably steepen. If he transferred his own weigh forward he might never shift Jim from the controls. The dive might become too steep.

Carol didn't know that, Bruce didn't know it, Mark didn't know it. They rained blows on him, they screamed at him to shift him from his seat, but they didn't understand that his hesitation was not cowardice. Even in the midst of his fright and indecision, Gerald knew that the aircraft was going to crash unless Jim pulled himself together. It would crash if Gerald failed to go to Jim's assistance, but it would just as surely crash if he did. Only

Jim could get them out of it.

'He's dead. He's dead. He's dead.'

It was Carol's voice, but it came from Jan, from the agonized framing of Jan's lips. She was crying, 'He's dead. He must be dead. Get up, Mr Jim. Oh, what am I to do? Get *up*, Mr Jim.'

It didn't matter any more. Nothing mattered very much. When death was as sure, as certain as this, did it matter whether is came in three minutes or two minutes or less? Gerald tore his seat harness away and plunged into the cockpit, stumbling over Colin, falling to his knees in sharp contact with the dead man's back. It was an awful sensation, even though a fleeting one; he seemed to have fallen against a sack of grain rather than against a man.

Gerald embraced the man and dragged frantically with strength of a kind he had never used before, well aware that he had only seconds before the dive became too steep. Jan, too, heaved up from her seat with a desperate convulsion of strength that she produced out of her weakness and her exhaustion, as a dying creature might use up its life force in a single effort. And the steepening dive did the rest; it didn't hold the body down; it ejected it. Suddenly, Jim came out like a cork from a bottle, almost over the top of Gerald, overbalancing the boy, pinning him against the door by his right arm and shoulder, but so frightening him, so revolting him, that he was pinned there for an instant only. Gerald recoiled from the weight of the dead man as from an electric shock. He saw then, in a vivid moment, that his left hand had closed fiercely over the back of the pilot's seat and that Jan was leaning towards him, both arms extended, her agitated fingers only inches from his face, her own face behind the fingers, beyond, stamped with the sort of expression he had never seen at any other time, on any face.

He snatched for her hands and felt fingers fasten on his wrist. He kicked, he scrambled, he clawed into the cockpit, and landed in the seat partly dazed and giddy, in a way marvelling that he had ever got there, in another way terrified that he had.

He had never held the controls except in straight and level flight, and this aircraft was going down, still going down, yawing from side to side, its attitude constantly changing, its instrument readings meaningless, and the pressures relayed from the wheel and the rudder bar wholly alarming, wholly confusing.

He didn't know where to begin. All he could see was red earth and a leaning horizon apparently above his head, a horizon that leaned first one way and then another. He didn't even know how high he was; couldn't find the altimeter on the instrument panel; couldn't think because of the screaming of the engine, the crying of the engine winding to a higher and higher note; couldn't reason because of fear, his own fear and the fear in the others. Their horror was an actual force, like a thing wrapping itself around him, not urging him to master the *Egret* with a calculated shuffling of hands and feet, but freezing him into helplessness, turning his muscles to stone and his limbs to unmoving, unyielding clay.

There was a pause, not in movement or in time or in events, but in the processes of Gerald's thoughts, a pause when nothing happened, when his only awareness was the dull and approaching certainty of death. It numbed him as though his body and brain had suffered a crushing physical blow. It held him motionless, transfixed, hypnotized, stiff-necked, and stiff-backed. His mouth was dry; his lips, parted, were stuck to his teeth. His eyes were rounded and protruding. He had become something solid, almost lifeless already; but the leaning horizon moved leisurely back and lay straight, high on the windscreen, and the slewing instrument needles steadied, and degree by degree, unseen by Gerald, the horizon crept down the windscreen like a slowly receding wave until it passed from sight and nothing was left but sky, pale sky, quite empty.

And the engine note changed; it was no longer screaming, no longer crying. It slid down and down the scale like a sigh.

And suddenly the boy felt blood in his veins, felt it thundering in his head, and he became aware of his mouth, of his tongue swollen, of his lips apparently cracking like oven-baked paper, of sweat starting in streams from his brow and armpits and back and abdomen and legs.

He saw the sky, nothing but sky, and heard the engine labouring as though panting up a steep hill, and felt the almost unbearable tension snap in his limbs.

His understanding leapt into the present. The aircraft was climbing far too steeply; struggling for lift, squashing, only a second or two short of the stall. This was something he knew. This was something he knew how to put right. His father, and Jim, too, had allowed him to reach the same position before.

Clumsily, but correctly, he edged the control column forward and the *Egret* sagged almost breathlessly and shook herself. There was a shudder in her wings, even in the floor, but the moment passed and the horizon came up and placed itself neatly above the base of the windscreen, just above the nose, almost exactly where it should have been.

Gerald realized it was there, not so much with amazement, but with awe. His father had always said that the *Egret* would fly herself if given half the chance, that a stable aeroplane was stable because of itself, not because of its pilot. If the controls were held at neutral, he maintained, then the *Egret*, like any good aeroplane, would sort out almost any tangle for herself. That was what he must have done! He must have held the controls at neutral or thereabouts, not because of what his father had said to him but because his fear had frozen him there.

Or was he being unfair to himself? In seconds, in flashes, his mind raced from conclusion to conclusion. Perhaps he had done it that way because his father had told him it was the right way. Perhaps he hadn't been frightened at all, not really. Perhaps his behaviour had demonstrated his presence of mind. Perhaps he had been master of the situation all the time. It was obvious, surely. A fellow couldn't fool himself about a thing like that. They were alive, weren't they, not dead? That should be proof enough for anybody.

He turned, then, to Jan, half expecting from her a smile or a warm and thankful hand, but Jan had been sick again. She was green. Funny, he had never noticed it before. Her face was like Bert's – common.

It was most disappointing and quite disgusting.

6. To the Wild Sky

Carol was ill; not air-sick or anything like that, but shaking uncontrollably and sobbing, frightening Bruce, bewildering Mark. She was shaking all over: her hands pressed to her eyes, her sun-glasses like bird's wings broken beneath her feet.

For a while she had been all right, no more terrified than the others, no more shocked than they were, no more helpless, but something had given way when it was all over.

She had tried so hard to stop it because she was not a baby. When it got down to things like real merit of character she was far stronger than many grown-ups. It was because of Jim mainly. She had never been confronted by death before and she sobbed at the indignity of it, for the way a nice man with nice eyes and a clean square jaw had been thrown aside by children when the spark of his life had gone out, when his usefulness had come to an end.

Bruce couldn't console her, though he tried, because he didn't really know what it was about. He knew it was Jim, but he didn't know in what way. He was upset, too, but girls were different from boys. His mother was always ramming that down his throat and he had come to accept it years ago, because Jan was his sister. She'd been born the same day, a twin with a brain that got much the same things right and much the same things wrong – but they had different hearts; one the heart of a boy, the other the heart of a girl.

Something drew Bruce's eyes to the front. It was Gerald, looking back from the cockpit. It was uncommonly difficult to see his face, for it was indistinct, almost hazed. Yet it was only seven or eight feet away. There seemed to be a smile on Gerald's face that said, 'Look what I've done! Aren't I clever? You'd all be dead like Jim but for me.'

That was true enough, but it was odd how the slant of Gerald's head seemed to say it out loud; and it was odd how arrogant, how unnecessary it seemed to be. Bruce liked Gerald. At other times, Bruce thought Gerald was marvellous; clever and rich and *different*. Normally, he would never have criticized Gerald, unless someone else had put a critical thought into his head.

Bruce smiled back, awkwardly, but only with his mouth. He didn't feel like smiling inside. And Gerald turned his eyes to the front again, still with that odd slant to his head, and Bruce stared at the back of his neck, strangely ill-at-ease. Gerald had always said he could fly and Bruce had never questioned him. He'd never doubted, even when death had seemed so close, that Gerald would bring the *Egret* under control if he could get into the pilot's seat, with his hands to the wheel. And Gerald had done that; Gerald had done everything that Bruce had expected of him, even though he had been terribly slow to start. There was no cause to doubt Gerald now. How could he doubt a boy who had proved himself? But he wished he wouldn't sit with that slant to his head, that cocky slant, like a show-off. Not while Jim was behind him, dead, on the floor.

Bruce had to do something about Jim. Jim had to be covered up. It wasn't decent the way he was. When people died they were supposed to be private, shut away, with something over them. And it wasn't right that Colin should be down there with him. It wasn't decent the way Colin was, either. Poor old Col.

Poor old Jim. Fancy a fella dying like that. Out like a light. And flying an aeroplane, too. It was awfully careless of somebody. Surely if a fella had to die he could die in bed or while he was having his dinner or taking a walk or something. Fancy dying in an aeroplane. Crikey, if he'd died on the outward trip instead of the homeward one, no one would have been the wiser. If he'd been in an empty aeroplane he'd have crashed and everyone would have said that he'd been stunting or something.

But fancy dying at all? So sudden. So quick. Did people always die like that? Out like a light?

Bruce looked at Jim again. He had to lean forward to bring him into view. He wasn't frightened of him, but he was very sorry, very sad in a way, and Carol didn't help. If anything really worried him it was Carol and the way she was carrying on. She seemed to *feel* it so much. Perhaps girls always kicked up a fuss. Perhaps boys felt it that little bit less because they were different from girls. Mark wasn't crying, or didn't seem to be. He was sitting almost erect in his seat, with ashen cheeks and his mouth open, and his head turned a little to one side. But big, slow tears were channelling down the side of Mark's nose and were sharp on his tongue. He was so frightened. His heart thudded against his ribs, almost taking his breath away. He just couldn't believe that it had happened. Every time he tried to think of it, it overwhelmed him. But he was determined not to cry. He would die before he would cry. These tears weren't really crying. They were different. He wanted to ask Bruce: 'Can Gerald really fly? Will he get us there? And Jim's not really dead, is he? Not really *dead*?'

Gerald flew on, still getting the feel of things, still trying

to remember what all the different instruments meant.
Which lever, for instance, was throttle? Which was mix-
ture? Which was pitch? You could tell best by sense of
touch. Oh, it was easy enough to read the labels on the
throttle-box, but that was a mug's way of doing it. But the
instruments on the flying panel caused him most concern;
the rate-of-climb indicator for one. He couldn't get it back
to zero. Even when the horizon was level and the airspeed
more or less right, the *Egret* continued to climb at about
800 feet a minute. It had doubled its height in only a few
minutes. When everything had settled down, his height
had been 5,000 feet; now it was over 10,000, and the only
way he knew of getting down again was to push the nose
forward. But then the *Egret* started going faster and faster:
130 knots, 140 knots and then 150, and that was much too
fast. There was a metal plate riveted on to the instrument
panel that said:

Take-off	. .	50 knots
Climb	. .	90 knots
Cruise	. .	120 knots
Maximum	. .	140 knots
Glide	. .	90 knots
Stall	. .	40 knots

And then there was another batch of speeds for use with
flaps; quarter flap, half flap, three-quarter flap, full flap.
Flaps? Gerald didn't even know what to do with them.

It was very handy having all this information plastered
on notices round the cockpit, but it was worrying when
the figures wouldn't fit. He'd never worried about figures
before. When he had flown with his father, his father had
done all the worrying about that sort of thing. He was
always screaming at Gerald: 'Watch that airspeed. Watch

your altimeter. Can't you see your turn-and-bank? Look at your artificial horizon. For heaven's sake, boy; airspeed, airspeed. Now what course are you supposed to be flying? Not *that*. Check your gyro against your compass. Airspeed, airspeed! Do you want to kill the lot of us? Get out of that seat. Come on, out of it! You couldn't fly a kite.'

Sometimes it had been a blessed relief to get out of the seat, away from those fiendish instruments, but he couldn't get away now. Now there was no one beside him to take over; no one to scream and shout; no one to push the wheel forward or pull it back; no one to straighten it up when he dropped a wing; no one to adjust the throttle!

The throttle!

That's what it was. That was why he kept going up and up. Jim must have been climbing when he died, and the throttle hadn't been altered. It was still set for the climb.

But what sort of adjustment was it that he had to make? His father had always done it for him. He'd never noticed. He had always been so busy keeping the aircraft reasonably straight and level.

That was why everything was so noisy. The engine was set for the climb. Golly, if he climbed at the proper speed, at ninety knots, he'd be going up like a rocket. What the dickens was Jim climbing for at that rate?

He had to alter the throttle. It was no good looking to anyone else to do it for him. No one else aboard knew the first thing about it.

Gerald closed his eyes for a moment, tightly. He was not a fool. He knew the game was over. Just for a minute or two it had been a game, in a way; a big thrill. Just for a minute or two he had had a sense of power, of mastery, of absolute control.

It wasn't going to be as easy as that, because his arms were aching already and his legs to the rudder bar were trembling and there was this fear of touching anything, of altering anything, even the trim. That was why there was so much pressure on the wheel, that was why his arms were aching. The aircraft was *trimmed* for the climb. It was not only a matter of altering the throttle; the trimming tabs had to be adjusted, too, and probably the pitch of the propeller as well. Flying an aeroplane was so much more than holding a wheel. So very much more. There was even the danger of climbing so high that people would start getting sick, start fainting. People coming up quickly from lower levels were supposed to use oxygen over 10,000 feet and he was up to 12,000 already.

'Oh, Jim,' he groaned, 'What am I to do?'

As soon as one control was altered everything else had to be altered, too. He'd be pushing at this and pulling at that and he might never get things back into balance. The fact that everything had been balanced for the climb was the only reason the *Egret* was still in the air, instead of lying crushed on the plain. As things were, she would continue to climb but would remain stable. Once anything was altered, Jim's dead hand would cease to control it. One mistake would lead on to the next, then to the next, and finally to disaster.

The altimeter reached 13,000 feet and crept on farther round the dial. Gerald's hand had gone indecisively to the throttle lever; he had rested it there, but he just wasn't brave enough to draw back the throttle. He'd removed his hand, then replaced it, and taken it away yet again. Oh, how he wished for someone to help him; for the voice of a man to say, 'All right, son. Pull it back. If you get into trouble I'll put it right.' But there was no voice, no reassuring hand, no *presence*.

Perhaps he could edge it back a little, a minute amount. Surely that wouldn't upset everything? After all, he was holding the nose down now, against the pressure of the trim, and managing it all right, even if his arms were tiring. Golly. That was something he mustn't forget. He mustn't tire himself out. There was no automatic pilot on the *Egret* – not that he would have known how to use it. Oh, glory. The complications. Was there no end to them?

The altimeter read 14,200 feet, far higher than he had ever been in the *Egret* before; far, far higher.

If he did throttle back, the trim would still be wrong, quite wrong, and he'd have to hold the nose up. Then he'd lose airspeed and the slower the *Egret* flew the harder she would be to handle. Speed was safety. He had started talking to himself and didn't realize it. And there were hours still to go, no radio to send a distress signal, and Coonabibba homestead to find!

He peered down, almost with a touch of giddiness. The ground seemed to be a thousand miles away, a blur, meaningless, featureless, endlessly flat, endlessly monotonous, no rivers, no roads, no hills, no big broad arrows saying, 'This way to Coonabibba'.

Gerald looked away, right away from it. It frightened him and weakened him. His breathing was quickening, a dull ache was gathering in his ears and his eyes were playing tricks. They must be, otherwise he'd surely be able to see something on the ground and the sky would be blue, not white. Even the sun had paled.

Cloud! He was flying into cloud, brushing at the edges of it, cloud like mist on a pond, acres of it, miles of it. Cloud in layers like magic carpets for as far as he could see.

He whimpered. He knew he would never fly blind. In cloud he would lose his balance. There was an almost irresistible impulse to drag the throttle off and drop away from it all, but he was too scared. His fear was even stronger than his impulse.

'What am I to do?' He cried it out, screamed at the windscreen, and, distraught, turned suddenly on Jan. 'What am I to do? I don't know what to do.' But Jan was huddled in her seat, dull of eye and disinterested. She looked almost stupid. He had half hoped for a miracle, that he'd find his father sitting there, but instead it was a stupid, slow-witted, heavy-lidded girl shivering from head to foot. He detested her. Jim should have been there. Yes, Jim. It was unfair. It was crazy. Jim *should* have been there. It was his job to have been there. He was paid good money to be there.

He shouldn't be down on the floor, not down near the door. What the dickens was Bruce doing with him? Bruce shouldn't have left his seat. Jim had particularly asked him not to do so. What did Bruce mean by moving around? Bruce was in his shirt, looking frozen. Laboriously, as though his coat weighed a ton, he placed it over Jim's head. His eyes, wide eyes, looked up and his lips formed the word, 'Cold!'

Ridiculous. Was there no end to the silliness of people? Cold? What did cold have to do with it? How could Jim be cold on a beautiful day like this?

Gerald sneaked a look at the altimeter again. He had been trying not to. He hadn't looked at it for quite a while. For how long? One minute? Ten minutes? A timeless interval. 17,300 feet and not a mountain to cross. He peered closer. Perhaps it was upside down. In that instant sunlight vanished and the *Egret* shook. It was as though she had run over a bump in a road.

Gerald blinked, dazed, sleepy. His ears were hurting. His feet and toes were numb. Ahead was nothing. Blankness. Emptiness. He lurched to the side to look down, but the earth had gone. The sun had gone, too. Imagine that? And he felt sick, in a vague sort of way, and sore and short of breath. He could have been struggling in mud or drowning in ice.

It was so cold and bleak. It was winter-time, but everything was wrong. Something in him clung desperately to that thought. The only thing right was the knob of the throttle lever hot against the palm of his hand. Everything else was cold. Even his hand was cold, but the knob of the throttle lever was like the bowl of his father's pipe, warm and reassuring. He knew that something had to be done with the throttle, something he hadn't wanted to do.

He pushed it. It was faintly surprising how strongly it resisted him, but the engine responded. He heard its roar gather more power but then a voice said to him, 'That's not right, either.' So he pulled it back again and something seemed to be cut away from beneath him. He seemed to be sitting in mid-air. He seemed to be suspended. It was a funny feeling. The engine note had receded as though it had gone away somewhere; into another room, perhaps, or round the corner of the street.

After a while he got used to it and rather liked the sound of it. It sounded like the rhythm of a dance-band, though sometimes it was as though the drummer lost the beat and thrashed about a bit. Then, just when Gerald thought he had lost it completely, the rhythm would come in again. That happened several times. And there was another sound, as though there were two drummers, one with sticks and the other with a switch, and gradually the one with the switch became stronger. It was a rushing sound, like water or wind, or the toboggan that had swept him down the mountainside at the snowfields last year.

Then it sounded like the *Egret* in the hands of his father as it turned into wind for landing, as it glided steeply with the engine throttled back towards the dusty red earth, half a mile from the homestead. But his father wasn't there and the homestead wasn't there and the earth wasn't there either. All the world was grey except for a red mist below. Cloud above him, open air around him, and wind-driven dust beneath. And 9,400 feet on the altimeter.

Gerald was very calm, as though an invisible hand stroked his brow. The *Egret* was controlled; she was not plunging wildly towards earth. She was dropping at a hundred knots and dropping straight.

The boy thought back, but there were recent minutes of some obscurity. He could remember them, but not clearly. Yet something had happened. He had entered those minutes in a state of terror; he had emerged from them self-possessed. He was so sore all over, inside and outside, but he was calm.

His father had thrashed him once with straight-faced and unwavering severity, and afterwards Gerald had been calm. He had known why he had been thrashed and it made sense. This made sense, too. In a way, he had been thrashed again. And now he was calm; confident enough to allow the *Egret* to continue its downward path; humbled enough to regard his former self with some distaste.

It was senseless trying to forget that the throttle existed. He *had* to use it and he would never begin to understand its operation until he did use it. The idea was to use it very gently, a little at a time. He had to do the same with the trimming tabs – a little at a time. Everything in the cockpit, in fact, had to be handled that way; then, with any sort of luck, he should be able to keep out of serious trouble. No more of this business of getting above 10,000 feet, nor of getting below 5,000, either. At one extreme of height there were the curious dangers of rarefied air and at the other extreme he would be too close to the hard ground to correct mistakes. All he had to do was to remain safely in the air and practise the different drills. He could even practise landing in the air, up to a point. He had to keep his head and take his time. There was all the time in the world. The *Egret's* tanks were almost full; she certainly carried sixty gallons; and that gave him six hours in the air. No; it didn't give him six hours. That would take him on to 8 p.m. and it would be dark sometime between 7.00 and 7.30. So he had five hours in which to prepare himself for landing.

Six thousand feet. Time to start working on the throttle.

He advanced it a fraction, judged its effect, and advanced it a bit more. It wasn't difficult. By the time the aircraft was down to 4,700 feet he had found the balance between engine power and level flight, and very cautiously had reached up his hand for the trimming tabs. He started turning the handle, first the wrong way. There was no mistaking that build-up of pressure in the flying controls, so he wound the other way, and little by little the pressure eased out. It was a *marvellous* feeling. It was such a relief, such a thrill. He couldn't remember anything, ever, that had given him a greater sense of well-being and satisfaction. He had to smile. He couldn't help himself. But there wasn't arrogance in his smile now. That had gone; the cocky slant to his head had gone, too. His pride now wasn't for himself; it was for the *Egret*. He felt a sudden affection for her, different from what he had known before, something like the affection one had for a friend as distinct from the feeling one might have had for a possession. The *Egret* was working for him, just as she worked for his father, just as she had worked for Jim; even though Gerald knew the propeller pitch was not quite right. The *Egret* was working for him, despite that. She had made allowances for him. She was on his side. And it was not that conditions were good. The air was disturbed and she was moving around a lot but she always came back to an even keel. Even when the bumps were bad and she dropped a wing, he tried not to help her too much. 'Let her fly herself.' It was his own voice, his inner voice, but they were his father's words.

Of course he still had to find Coonabibba. That wasn't going to be easy. But there was time, time enough. And when he found it, he would circle and make a few runs over the homestead and drop a note. Yes, a note, telling them what had happened. Then he'd give them time to get out to the strip and to make everything ready for a crash landing. He tightened a little when he thought of the landing, but the certainty of a very heavy, very rough touchdown had to be faced. It was good that the *Egret* was rugged; it was good that she could take punishment, for she would certainly have to take it this day. Landing wasn't easy. Landing was the hardest job any pilot had to do. Even good pilots made bad landings sometimes; bad pilots made good landings hardly ever.

Gerald looked over the side, looked down, half expecting to see the River Darling near Louth. They usually crossed the river within sight of Louth. It was the one landmark that Gerald could be sure of. There wasn't much else he could identify with certainty; one boundary fence looked the same as another, one homestead the same as another, one station track the same as another; but Louth was unmistakable.

But the Darling wasn't there. There was no river. There was nothing.

That struck a chord in him, even if it startled him. He had seen the dust before, but in some odd way its significance had not registered. The dust wasn't lying in clouds, not exactly; it was a haze, like a filmy curtain laid over the land. There were a few shadows beyond the curtain, a few irregular shapes, probably earth of changing colours or vegetation of different kinds, but nothing recognizable. Certainly no river. Not anywhere.

Gerald thought about it, and step by step, moment by moment, an awareness of danger of the gravest kind shaped up in his mind. The aircraft was working for him, it wasn't fighting against him, but he had let it down. He had made a calamitous mistake.

Not once, not from the instant that he had assumed control, had he consciously attempted to fly in a straight line. He didn't even know what heading he was supposed to be flying.

Gerald sank back in his seat, appalled. He had been flying round the sky for half an hour, perhaps longer, without once checking his course. And you couldn't do that sort of thing in an aeroplane. Why, he had heard that echo of his father's words: 'Check your gyro against your compass!' – and had failed to act upon it. He had been worrying about height, about throttle, about pitch, about trim, about practically everything in the cockpit except the compass.

He was afraid to look at it – at the compass or the directional gyro.

Oh, what a shocking thing to have done.

What a stupid, stupid thing to have done.

He forced himself to look down to the compass mounted on the side of the cockpit close to his left knee, and the needle was lying across the grid lines, not parallel to them as it should have been. He was just about as far off-course as it was possible to get, short of turning round and flying in the opposite direction.

If Jim had set the course! Perhaps he hadn't done so. Jim mightn't have bothered; he might have been flying by eye, by instinct, map-reading his way along from landmark to landmark. There was a map, too, on the floor at the base of the seat, probably where it had slipped from Jim's lap.

The course set on the compass was 250 degrees. The course Gerald was flying was about 100 degrees off it. Which way? Here was a block. Which way should he read an aircraft compass? He couldn't say, not with certainty, for he had never had to read a compass with accuracy. His father had always checked the course. But 250 degrees – even if he had been steering it – couldn't take him to Coonabibba. Impossible. 250 degrees was roughly south-west. Coonabibba was north-west. His fears were well grounded. Jim had not set the course!

Or had he? Perhaps there was something else that he hadn't reckoned on. Quietly, now, quietly. Work it out.

How did a pilot set a course?

Oh, there were so many things that Gerald didn't know; so many mysteries; so many perfectly ordinary things that he had never bothered to inquire about.

What influenced the heading of an aircraft? Of course, wind! And something else; variation, or deviation – a word something like that, but what did it mean? Could wind and variation – whatever that was – cause a pilot to steer south-west instead of north-west? Surely not.

Gerald shivered. This was awful. Jim hadn't set the course, unless there were factors that Gerald could not account for.

He looked down again into the dust haze. There was a real wind blowing down there, half a gale at least. Was it blowing up here, too? How was he to find out? If he couldn't see the ground, how could he tell? Oh, golly, golly, golly. This meant they were lost. Not just half-lost, either. There'd be no landing at Coonabibba.

Of that there wasn't a hope in the world. Not by inventing all sorts of fancies, all sorts of miracles, could he expect to find Coonabibba, for even if he flew over it he wouldn't know it was there. He wouldn't be able to see it for dust.

He had to keep his head. They might be lost but they weren't doomed to die. He had to look for some other station, some other homestead, and land as soon as he could before the dust got worse. There was no need to panic. In fact, the dangers were no greater than before. The only real danger was landing, and that danger became no greater or less because it had to happen at Point B instead of Point A. He could still fly over the homestead, any homestead, and buzz it, still drop a note, still wait until they were ready for him. Then the people could send a message to Coonabibba to let them know that everything was all right. After all, the Hennessys knew everybody in

the west. Everybody knew everybody else. No matter where
he landed he would be sure to find friends.

Well then? What course should he fly? North-west, he
supposed. At least that would take him into his own part
of the country. Obviously he should aim to come down
as close to Coonabibba as he could.

Gerald looked carefully at the compass, then reached
down, unclamped it, and turned the ring until 315 degrees
came up against the arrow. He was not a great distance
off-course, after all. There he locked it, and little by little
skidded the aircraft round until the compass needle lay
between the parallel lines of the grid. It took a very long
time. It was really quite extraordinary. The needle played
the most peculiar tricks. It didn't turn at the same rate
as the aircraft. Sometimes it went faster, sometimes slower.
Time and again he thought he had it right, but then a
few moments later the needle would swing off again, to
one side or the other, by as much as ten or fifteen degrees.
He tried to make it easier by using the directional gyro,
but the figures didn't make sense. It was so hard to read
the gyro.

After a while he looked at the clock and it was 2.38.
There must have been something wrong with the thing.
He couldn't have taken more than half an hour to alter
course. The very thought was absurd. He checked it against
his wrist-watch. The clock was correct. Then he remembered the altimeter. It registered 8,700 feet.

He felt a flutter of the old concern, of the old panic,
but resolutely stifled it and gently closed the throttle until
the *Egret* began unmistakably to descend. By then he was
twenty degrees off-course again and his airspeed had
slipped back to seventy knots.

7. Flying into Nowhere

Gerald had changed. Bruce could see that; Bruce had known it for a long time. Gerald wasn't arrogant any more. Gerald was a boy again; the sort of boy that Bruce had always liked. Perhaps *courageous* was the word that Bruce was thinking of.

Gerald was hunched in the cockpit wholly engrossed, like the driver of a racing car or an express train. There wasn't a thought in his head except the needs of the *Egret*. Bruce could see that; no one else in the aircraft existed to Gerald. He was alone. Jan was beside him apparently asleep or exhausted, so close that Gerald perhaps could have woken her simply by looking at her, but not once did he turn to her. Not once did he turn back to look at the others in the cabin. Nor glance at Jim. (Bruce wished that he would turn round. He had a longing, an almost insatiable curiosity to see his face.)

Gerald remained hunched, occasionally reaching out an arm to this control or that, sometimes leaning forward to peer at the instrument panel. Sometimes he leant to the window at his side and appeared to look down. Sometimes he sat erect and appeared to look ahead. But always he returned into the pit of his seat, slumped, hunched, as though trying to rest himself, as though trying to support his arms by his elbows, and his legs by the back of his thighs. That was just how he looked; like somebody who was trying to conserve his strength, or perhaps somebody concentrating desperately, trying to pass a too difficult examination.

Bruce knew that there was trouble, very big trouble. No one had told him; this was something that a fellow *knew*, perhaps not all fellows, but to fellows with intuition like Bruce's certain truths were apparent. Bruce always knew, for instance, when a fellow was lying, or when a teacher at school had made a wrong statement and was trying to get out of it, or when his Mum was working up to the point of telling him that girls were different from boys. Jan had weird and wonderful dreams and Mum said she was psychic; but Bruce *knew* things and Mum said he was impossible. Maybe that was one of the differences between boys and girls.

But Bruce knew now that Gerald was in trouble. He looked like a boy fighting grimly for something that he believed in. That was a new thought for Bruce, an angle on life he had not considered before. Gerald was in trouble, but he wasn't giving up, he wasn't giving in; he was *fighting*. Not with his fists, not putting on a big show or anything like that, but fighting with his heart and his will and with a slant to his head that no longer expressed arrogance. That slant meant determination. It meant, 'I will! I will!'

Bruce warmed to Gerald; continually warmed to him. It was a thrilling feeling, this whole-hearted, unselfish admiration for someone else, and the fact that Gerald had forgotten that Bruce existed didn't spoil it in the least. In a way it was like being invisible, like drifting round in mid-air in a curl of smoke *watching* people, but not being seen oneself. He felt he was seeing Gerald as maybe God would see him. That was a strange thought, but it seemed valid, it was like that; it really was.

Gerald was lost. Bruce knew that, too. He had only to

stretch himself and squint through the window to prove
it. That was dust down there and cloud up on top. It was
a sandwich and the *Egret* was in the middle. It was a
chicken sandwich, and the *Egret* was the chicken and what
chicken in a sandwich ever knew where it was going? Bruce
played with that thought for a while, then got round to
wondering who would eat the sandwich?

Where would they end up? Where would they land if
they couldn't find Coonabibba? Would the cloud come
down and the dust come up? Would they get squashed in
the middle and be able to see nothing at all? It wouldn't
be a sandwich then; it'd be a stew. Perhaps they'd crash.
Perhaps they'd fly into a mountain. Perhaps they'd go on
and on for ever and ever and vanish in the mists of time.
It wasn't funny, really. It was very, very serious. But Bruce
couldn't get worried about it. He felt he should have been
worried – if only to relieve Gerald of a little of his worries
– but his mind refused to work that way. He could see all
the dangers very clearly, but try as he would he couldn't
get upset about them.

He could see that no one could help them, that they
were on their own; but it didn't frighten him. He supposed it all came back to his faith in Gerald, to that tall,
slender, narrow-shouldered boy hunched in the pilot's
seat. This was Gerald's party in more ways than one. It
simply wasn't Bruce's party any more than it was Carol's
or Colin's.

Colin was still out to it, though Bruce had managed to
get him into Gerald's empty seat. Colin was no good for
company, nor was Carol. All red-eyed and tear-stained,
she was still huddled in her seat with a handkerchief held
to her nose, still sobbing once in a while for no apparent
reason. She made him mad. All dolled up as though she
was off to church, or to the races maybe, but snivelling all

the time. On and off she'd been snivelling for a couple of hours. She was pretty, Bruce supposed, in the way that girls sometimes were, but what a blooming mess she looked. As though she'd been dragged through a bush backwards. And for what? There was old Gerald up there, *fighting*, because Jim was dead; but Carol was snivelling for the same reason. And Jan? He wasn't quite sure what to think about Jan. If she hadn't helped to get Jim out of the seat they'd never have got him out, and if she hadn't helped Gerald to get into it they'd never have got him in, but surely she could take an interest in things. He was sure she wasn't asleep. She was keeping her eyes shut because she didn't want to look. Jan was an ostrich. And Mark was a pest.

Really and truly, someone should take that kid out and drown him. Shout, shout, shout. Jumping up and down all the time. Jigging around as though he had ants in his pants. Honest to goodness, you'd think that he'd have worn himself to a frazzle an hour ago. Having Jan for a sister was bad enough; having this little horror for a brother would be just about the end. Maybe that was why Col was such a quiet type; the poor fellow was probably beaten half stupid with noise. Probably Col was shamming, too. Probably keeping his eyes shut and his ears shut out of sheer exhaustion. Poor old Col. He sure looked terrible. He'd be in for some shocks when he woke up. Col didn't know about Jim. Didn't know about old Gerald up there, fighting. Didn't know about the climb, either, that had just about frozen everybody solid, or about the dust.

That dust was bad; getting worse, if anything. How was old Gerald *ever* to find Coonabibba? Three hours to Coonabibba, Jim had said. Only fifteen minutes to go, but everywhere there was only dust. The ground wasn't there. It had melted away.

There were no landmarks, no water-courses either dried
up or flowing, no artesian bores or tanks in little oases of
trees, no homesteads. Gerald peered into the dust haze
until his eyes smarted, until his brain was weary, until he
ached with foreboding, but saw nothing.

He hardened his resolve and took the *Egret* down to
2,000 feet (though bodily tired he was handling the controls with more confidence), but still saw nothing. And he
was afraid of hills. There weren't many, but there were
some. And he might not be near Coonabibba, anyway. He
might be farther west, near the ranges on the South Australian border, or farther south, near the ranges round
Broken Hill, or farther north, near the Queensland ranges,
or even west. And in the east there were great mountains.
There was no saying where he really was, no knowing, no
guessing. He hadn't seen a mark on the ground that he
could recognize for two and a half hours. And though he
had stuck on course, on 315, or as close to it as he could, it
was not the course that he was flying that determined his
position, but the unknown gale that was raising dust even
to 2,000 feet above the earth. He could have been almost
anywhere over the state of New South Wales or across its
borders.

Nor could he be sure that the altimeter was right. Altimeter readings varied according to the weather. Although
the altimeter said 2,000 feet, he might have been 3,000 feet
above the invisible ground. On the other hand he might
have been only 1,000 feet above it. There was no safe way
of finding out, and if this were Coonabibba country, hills
were lurking in the dust to heights greater than 1,000
feet; age-worn, flat-topped hills that on a clear day and
from a distance looked like picnic tables set for giants. On
a day like this, though, they were walls of crumbling rock

that might be met head-on, that might smash an aeroplane into tiny bits and pieces in a rending instant of time.

Was he to press down lower and lower, taking a chance on finding flat ground, on landing in a gale without people standing by to help if he crashed, or on coming down in wild country hundreds of miles from the nearest homestead?

There was nothing that he could do except fly on and on and on and wait for the dust to clear. But it was after four o'clock and what dust storm ever cleared in two or three hours? It would have to get worse before it got better, and in three hours' time it would be dark. There'd still be fuel left, enough to last another hour beyond that, but what was the use of fuel after dark? He couldn't land in the dark. Even at a proper aerodrome, with lights and everything, he wouldn't be able to land in the dark. He didn't know how. He'd have to be able to see! To take his sight away was to take his life away.

What course was he to fly? If the winds were set in such a way that he was actually tracking over the ground on 315 he might end up over the deserts, the real deserts of rock and salt and sand, and if he landed there no one would ever find them. No one lived out there, not even animals or birds, or so he had been told. It hadn't rained out there for years, except for a shower or two the Christmas before last.

If he turned south he would be sure to fly into the range country. He would have to go up to be safe, and the higher he went the less chance he would have of sighting a homestead or an area of level ground. It would be a case of sight by chance and swoop without delay. That was unlikely above 3,000 feet. The dust would have obscured his sighting before he could take advantage of it.

The same applied to the east. That was where the mountains were. They might be hundreds of miles away but they might be very close. He might run out of the dust sooner in that direction, but who was to say that he would? Who was to say that the dust would not hide the mountains until the moment that he hit them?

He had to fly north or he had to fly in a circle, one or the other. There were ranges north of Coonabibba, certainly there were, but he could fly for hundreds of miles in that direction before the hills became mountains. No matter where he was, or so he reasoned, he could fly north in comparative safety until dusk. Heading in that direction, providing he was above 2,000 feet, he could not possibly come to grief on high land. But if he chose to fly a circle he would be flying in all directions continuously, drifting with the wind, perhaps into the gravest danger.

He had to fly north.

He had to fly away into heaven alone knew what, because he dared not do anything else. Dared not even go down, groping for the ground, hoping for a miracle, hoping for the homestead, for any homestead to appear like a harbour bar after a rough crossing.

Gerald set 000 degrees on the compass and eventually settled on course, due north, though he knew that if the wind was on his port beam he still could be drifting east into the mountains, and if it was on his starboard beam he still could be drifting west into the desert. That was the chance he had to take. There was no way under the sun of avoiding it.

At five-twenty-one, Colin stirred weakly in his seat and opened his eyes. He had stirred several times during the past hour – as Jan had – but he had dropped off again, breathing heavily, rasping through the side of his mouth, his face still bloodless; even his hands crossed limply in his lap were grey, as though the long summer had not touched them.

He felt foul. His throat was hot and dry, his tongue was like a piece of leather. He longed to swallow, but couldn't; longed for a drink of water, longed for a cool bath. He wasn't a thinking creature at all, just a feeling one. He felt as though he had slept for a long day, exposed to the hot sun, as though heat had wrung the last drop of moisture out of his body.

For a while he stared at his blurred hands in his lap, unable to account for his attitude or for the noise that hammered at him, unable to remember why he should feel so ill, so absolutely wretched. Then he remembered; and an awful sensation of nausea swept through him. He fought it off grimly and his eyes shifted from his lap to the curious shape on the floor that looked rather like a man but couldn't have been.

It was covered with a coat, but it had the legs of a man.

Colin stared at it and heard a shrill voice at his ear. 'It's Jim. He's dead.'

It was Carol. He couldn't see her very well, because she was too close. Either she was raving mad or he was dreaming. That was Gerald up in front, flying. There was cloud outside, an endless ocean of cloud stretching to the limits of visibility. They were riding over the top of it as they would skim on skis across snow or sea. It *was* a dream.

But there were the unquestionable matters of reality; the vibration of the engine and the sound of it, the movement of the aircraft and the presence of it, the smells, the sensations of flight, the existence of himself, and the sun. That great big sun hanging low over the clouds was hot and real.

That meant Jim was there, dead. It meant Gerald was there, flying. It meant that he had slept for a long time while terrible things had happened.

He saw the water-bag in the bracket on the wall and groped for it. When he closed his hand over it and felt it, damp and cold, he knew that everything truly was real. He fumbled for the neck of the bag and for the plastic beaker and lifted them into his lap.

'Careful,' Carol cried. 'Don't spill it.'

He peered at her, trying to put her words together, trying to get the sense of them. Water was important. That was the meaning that came through to him. He nodded and gave her the bag then held the beaker out to her with a silent appeal. She half-filled it for him but wouldn't give him any more, shaking her head firmly, with pursed lips and narrowed eyes.

He made the water last, made it go as far as a pint, holding it in his mouth, barely allowing it to trickle down his throat. Colin had got the message. He was a bright boy. His scattered senses were coming together, were pin-pointing. No one had to tell Colin that they were lost; that if they were to have reached Coonabibba they would have done so one hour and fifteen minutes ago. No one had to tell him that that ocean of cloud cut them off from the earth. It might as well have been an ocean of rock. It was impregnable. No aeroplane flown by a boy would ever get down through it.

Everything was so terrifyingly clear to Colin. Even the sun. The sun wasn't right. It didn't look like his sun. It looked like a sun that belonged somewhere else, that shone over an alien world.

Then the water turned his stomach and he was sick again and his vision clouded over and his brain dulled and the one boy aboard who might have had the mind and the ingenuity to grapple with figures and angles, with courses and with winds, lapsed again into uselessness.

Gerald had run into cloud shortly before five o'clock. It had pressed down and down until he had had no choice but to steel himself to fly up through it. He had gone up through it on instruments for twelve fearful, almost endless minutes, and had broken out into glorious sunlight at 11,000 feet. By then his nerve had been close to breaking point. Looking back, he marvelled that he had had the courage or the resolve or the ability. Almost numbed with fear he had set the *Egret* for the climb and allowed her to climb, allowed her to feel her way up, allowed her to fly herself. How he loved her. She was beautiful. She was marvellous. Oh, she was working so hard for him. It wouldn't be her fault if they came to a sticky end.

It was after he had got there, after he had sat himself on top of the cloud, that he had started thinking about ice. Oh, golly; if he had thought of it sooner he would never have got through to 11,000 feet. He'd have turned back. He could so easily have iced-up in that cloud. His controls would have frozen, his engine would have choked out, and they would have plunged in terror to their deaths. There were ways of beating ice and the *Egret* could beat it, but only if one knew which buttons to push, which switches to turn. Gerald knew now, he had read round the cockpit until he had found them, but during the climb he had not known. How dangerous a little knowledge could be. How often the gods had smiled upon his ignorance when they should have struck him down. Oh, she was a lucky aircraft, the *Egret*. She always had been. She'd never failed, never faltered. Not in four years and two months, from the day that Gerald's father had bought her and flown her proudly home to Coonabibba.

But what was happening down below?

What changes were passing across the face of the unseen countryside? Were there deserts down there, or pastures, or mountains, or towns? Was there a dusty silence or a roaring storm, tossing trees and driving rain? Or were there people occupied by their own work and their own thoughts, unaware of the helpless children two miles above them flying into nowhere? Or perhaps cocking their ears, listening?

They wouldn't be working now, if they were in towns. Shops would be shutting their doors because it was five-thirty exactly. Office workers would have gone home. Boys and girls would be listening to the children's hour or watching T.V. Mothers would be preparing the evening meal. Fish would be frying. Steaks would be grilling. There would be onions in the pan.

Gerald was so hungry. And tired. He ached and ached. His arms were so heavy. His legs felt as though they were breaking in two through the shins. Never, since the day of his birth, had each hour been so long. For nearly four hours now he had sat in this seat, wavering between terror and nerveless calm, adding up miles, or trying to add them up. It was so difficult to fly and calculate in figures at the same time. At 120 knots, how many miles did he cover in an hour? Give or take a few, he thought about 140. Multiplied by four hours that made 560, multiplied by five hours it made 700, and by six hours about 850. Then there were the periods when he had gone faster and the periods when he had gone slower, the periods when he had wavered about trying to settle on course, the long beginning when he had flown no set course at all. And the wind! That was the vital reckoning. Depending upon its direction, the speed of the wind had to be added on or taken off. After six hours aloft, by which time he would have to land somehow, he might have covered over the ground less than 500 miles or more than 1,000, or any intermediate distance. He *couldn't* reckon it up. He got lost in its byways.

Glory, a thousand miles? Where would that put him? Into the dead heart of the continent or into the sea?

What if he broke cloud over the sea?

What sea would it be and in what direction would the land lie?

He was imagining things again. Pilots shouldn't have over-active imaginations. It was a stupid and dangerous thought. It was the sort of thought that could lead to a panic decision to push down into the unknown, through the cloud, looking for the ground. He had to resist that temptation. Indeed, he had to resist the temptation to think of anything that he feared. That sort of thinking was sabotage. Anything that affected his nerve or his confidence was a threat to the lives of six people.

More and more he was becoming aware of those people, those children, his friends. They'd been marvellous. They really had. They must have been frightened half out of their wits, but they had kept their places, hadn't been near him, hadn't bothered him, hadn't interfered in any way at all. A fellow could be lucky with his friends. Or perhaps with Bruce. It was probably Bruce.

He turned his back for the first time in hours and immediately met Bruce's eyes and Carol's too. He smiled at them and they waved.

Gerald warmed inside.

They were marvellous friends; marvellous the way they had trusted him.

He glanced at Jan, at that funny little girl huddled in the right-hand seat, and for an instant caught her bloodshot eye peeping at him round her nose. In the same instant the eye shut. Poor kid. She was so sick.

He owed it to them all to keep his mind off things that frightened him. It was better simply to fly, to put his faith in the lucky *Egret* and to fix his thoughts upon the certainty of a safe arrival somewhere.

He had to fly on until the sky was clear and the earth was laid out in order and clarity beneath him. And all the time, despite everything, he had to admit to the conviction that when the cloud parted, as soon it surely would, he would find an open road to land on or a town with an air-strip or a homestead paddock, flat and wide waiting for him. Upon that picture he had to freeze his thoughts and dismiss every unhappy alternative.

The moon rose to the lip of the cloud at a minute after six o'clock and the sun set at 6.08.

There should be an hour's twilight, or thereabouts. That was what Gerald thought. It was what Bruce thought. Not that either of them had ever put a stop-watch on twilight before. It was one of those things that you lived with, that you took for granted, that seemed to last about an hour towards the end of summer. Of course, it was not a period of undiminished light, it was a period of fading light, of dying light, which at a certain point rather difficult to determine it ceased to be light and became darkness.

There was no break in the cloud. Ten-tenths cloud, pilots called it. Its upper surface was like the sea on a choppy day. It was like the sea along a rocky coast, here and there breaking over reefs with towers of spray, with forms like ships of another day sailing past with rose-tinted canvas blooming to the wind. But remarkably level for all that; not often below 10,000 feet, rarely above 12,000 feet.

But it was thick and deep; thousands of feet deep. It was still a barrier that would not allow Gerald to go down.

Bruce knew that. Cloud was their enemy, just as much as the dust had been, but a distinct anxiety was beginning to take root in Bruce. Would the cloud be gone before dark? The optimism in his nature said it would, but a streak of pessimism, foreign to him, said it wouldn't. What then? Would the light of the moon be light enough to fly by and to land by? It was a half moon, maybe about five-eighths. It was a clear moon, already bright and white. Would it be bright enough for Gerald to see by?

What was Gerald thinking about? Bruce felt he should be sitting in that seat beside Gerald. Back here he felt useless, but Jan was there and he'd never shift Jan. Ask her to move and she'd be sick all over the place again.

What was Jan thinking? She was far too restless to be sleeping; she was squirming in her seat, shifting from one side to the other. Bruised. Just as Bruce was bruised. He'd have to eat his dinner off the mantelpiece for a week. (Dinner? Crumbs, he was hungry.) And there was a chill in the air now that the sun had gone. It was surprising how quickly the difference was felt. Surprising, too, how rapidly the red lights, the pink lights and the purple lights were streaking in the sky, immense smudges of colour in motion, red in the west, pink and purple in the east. They were beautiful. It was the sort of sky you wanted to share with people, but how could you share it in silence with a sleepy looking individual like Mark? It was like being in solitary confinement, sitting next to Mark; cut off from everybody else by the sound of the engine and not game to shout anything in Mark's direction in case he shook himself out of his doze and started performing again. Bruce felt that Mark dozing, or sound asleep, was the only sort of Mark he'd ever be able to take.

Colin stirred again, lifting his head from Carol's shoulder. She had put his head there. Quite the little mother, now that she had stopped her snivelling, Bruce thought. But she was very tense. Her back was very straight. Bruce knew that Carol was scared stiff but he was too shy to reach over and hold her hand to reassure her, or anything like that. Now that Carol was more herself again she wasn't to be trifled with, not in thought or in deed. Bruce was always a bit wary of Carol; he felt she was out of his class. But it would have been nice to have had her to speak to. It was awful, this being cut off from everybody. They were all in solitary confinement, every one of them. And they'd had five hours of it, with a dead man on the floor.

Now Colin seemed to have pulled himself together. He was sitting up, looking around, looking at the evening light. More than a little concerned, Colin seemed to be. But Colin was like that. His normally serious demeanour gave to really serious events a very grave tone indeed. Colin had an accountant's face; that was what Bruce's father said. It was the finely chiselled sort of face that one day would probably wear spectacles without rims, and regard with polite concern but acute perception from behind a broad desk (marked C. J. Martin, Manager) the wiles of hopeful clients seeking to increase their bank overdrafts. Yes, that was what Bruce's father said. Bruce himself had been left a bit vague as to his meaning.

But Colin was sitting up now, in a careful sort of way, looking at the evening light. Just looking. At the purples and the leaden greys and the icy blues and the dying flush in the ocean of cloud. So seriously.

Then it broke through to Bruce.

Night was coming. It truly was. There was a star in the sky.

But the sun had gone scarcely a quarter of an hour! It shouldn't be getting dark yet. It couldn't possibly happen. It must be the atmosphere; the cloud or something. Or the height. It must be a mistake.

Mark woke with a start, sat bolt upright, and yelled, 'What's up?'

And Jan was obviously awake. She made no pretence of feigning sleep any longer – or else the fading light had compelled her to face up to a reality that she had tried to hide from.

Gerald knew, too. He knew it in a way that the others did not. He knew that when light went, their lives went with it.

Why should night come so soon, so quickly? There were a hundred stars in the sky, the moon was brilliant, and gloom was coming up out of the east and north like a storm. He couldn't get to the ground, even if he tried. There wasn't time.

And there wasn't a break in the cloud, either. It was endless. It wasn't fair. It wasn't giving him a chance. Had he tried so hard, only to be beaten by an accident of Nature like this?

8. The Wings are Clipped

At six-thirty-five it was dark and the cloud was like a plain of pale silver in the moonlight.

Gerald still had a visible horizon to guide him, the line between cloud and sky, but the instruments distracted him. They were green and luminous, their pointers moving eerily to the variations of his flight. Maintaining a steady course was the hardest. He steered a wavering line that varied from side to side by as much as twenty degrees. Height was tricky, too. He would have been happier to have switched on the cabin lights, but the reflections on the windscreen would have cut him off from the faint horizon that he needed so much. He had tried it and almost instantly had lost his touch. He had felt giddy, unattached, as though pitched in mid-air from a fair-ground wheel. So he had to fly in darkness and his passengers had to sit in darkness, aware of each other as moon shadows, aware of Gerald as a dimly seen statue in the pilot's seat.

How much longer could it go on? Gerald knew; the others didn't. Unless his fuel consumption had varied greatly from the usual ten gallons an hour, he could stay up for ninety minutes more. Another ninety minutes, another 200 miles. Surely, surely it should be time enough and far enough for the cloud to break. By all the laws and averages it should have broken up long ago. Then the engine would splutter and race and cough and splutter again. And then it would stop.

And then?

Gerald tried not to think about it, tried to shut it out, but he couldn't.

Down through cloud and blackness without an engine to hold him, down the long path of a glide that could not be stopped ...

Gliding speed? What was it? Ninety knots. The same as climbing speed. Landing speed; what was that? Probably the same as stalling. Forty knots. They were figures he had to remember. Particularly landing speed. If he got it back to forty knots too high above the ground he'd crash. If he flew it into the ground at a speed above forty knots he'd crash just the same. And how was he to see the ground? It would be black as pitch down there beneath the cloud. And how was he to work out which way the wind was blowing? Because if he landed down-wind or across the wind he'd crash, too.

It couldn't be done. There were too many things against him. The student pilot had to make dozens of landings before he was allowed to fly solo, and Gerald had never made a landing, not of any kind, not even a roaring, bumping, boisterous one in broad daylight.

He had made a mistake. He should have headed for the ground like a bat out of hell as soon as he had seen that light was on the wane. Cloud or tempest, desert or forest, he should have got himself on to the ground. What did it matter if there were a few broken bones? Far better to crack a leg or an arm or even a skull than be smashed to pieces.

There was no break in the cloud. It was a pool of pale silver reaching to the end of the world. The end of the summer drought; that's what it was. The drought had broken; that was the story.

Rain would be belting down at Coonabibba. Coonabibba would be a sea of mud. Coonabibba would be a
house full of guests without Gerald or Carol or Colin or
Bruce or Jan or Mark. Or Jim.

It would be a house of fear. The telephone lines to the
out-stations would be running hot. They'd be out on
motor-bikes and horses and the blitz buggy. They'd be
calling the flying doctor and other homesteads and towns
and airports on the radio. And the rain would be thundering on the roof and his mother would be standing at the
window looking into the night.

And any minute now Bert would be listening to the
seven o'clock news and there'd be a report of the missing
Egret, and he would start thinking back over the nasty
things he had said. And perhaps he'd be sorry.

And tomorrow was Gerald's birthday. He'd probably
never see it. Probably never live to be fourteen. It wasn't
fair. And in a sort of way he would be dying by his own
hand. That was really awful.

Gliding speed was ninety knots. Landing speed was
forty knots. He might need them at any time. If his fooling
round with the engine had used more fuel than ten gallons
an hour the tanks might be all but empty. The fuel gauge
was way down but there were always a few gallons in reserve. He might be using the reserve now. The intricacies
of the fuel system he did not understand. He had to be
prepared for the symptoms of fuel starvation and engine
failure. They could strike at him at any time from now on.

He listened for the symptoms, waited for them, but the
Egret droned on and on.

Maybe he ought to pray for the cloud to break. It
couldn't do any harm. Or could it? If his prayer wasn't
answered he'd feel even more cut off, even more the victim
of a monstrous fate. The others would be praying, anyway.

They'd be praying their heads off. Jan, for one, would be calling on all the saints of Christendom. She was a bit that way inclined, was Jan. Maybe it was better in her hands than his. 'Praying's all right for parsons,' his father sometimes said. 'Speaking for myself I'd rather roll up my sleeves and rely on my own sweat.' That was all right up to a point, but it didn't seem to cover situations like this. Perhaps his father had never been in a situation like this.

'A break in the cloud,' said Gerald cautiously to the brightest star that he could see, 'would be very handy. Not that I'm putting a firm request or anything like that. But it would be handy. You appreciate my point of view; that if you don't bring along a break in the clouds, Jan here, who's probably praying for it like mad, will be awfully upset, because she's always been a bit of a one for taking you seriously. And I'll be upset, too, now that I've got round to asking you, when I didn't mean to. It's not that I come knocking on your door every time I've got a belly-ache. I mean, it's a bit hard for a fellow when his dad reckons it's strictly for the birds. And it's not as if I was asking only for myself; though I would like to be fourteen. I mean, if the cloud does break, it'll give me a fighting chance. It shouldn't be that hard for you. You must have ways . . .'

But the *Egret* droned on and on and the cloud did not break.

Perhaps he shouldn't have been so familiar; perhaps he should have done it more like they did it in church. The trouble was, he wasn't an authority on that sort of thing. He worried about it for a while and tried to say it in a more appropriate way, but got mixed up with the *dosts* and *doests* and *shouldests* and his mind fell silent, almost breathlessly, in a state of cold and lonely fear.

Jan saw it before anyone else. At about seven-thirty, at about the time when everyone was waiting for the engine to stop. No one had talked about fuel; what was the use of talking, anyway? But they all knew, even the girls, that engines which run on fuel have to run out of fuel some-time, and that the *Egret* just couldn't keep on going for ever. They seemed to have been sitting in this plane, im-prisoned, for days, waiting to die. Once night had come – so strangely and so swiftly – they had known that there wasn't much that Gerald could do any more. They didn't blame him, but something was strange just the same. Gerald just flew on and on as though he wanted to fly away to another world, almost as though he didn't want to go down, almost as though he didn't know how to go down.

They seemed to be flying away from everything they had ever known; school, home, mums and dads, friends, relations, and everything else that had added up to be their lives. It was the strangest feeling, as though they had shut a door behind them and stepped into emptiness. As though they had climbed into this aeroplane ages ago and had been in it ever since. As though, in some way, there had been a trick of time and they were its captives.

Jan saw it on her side, way out near the moon, a sort of blackness, like a shadow cast from something far above them. She watched it for a while, mainly because it was something different to look at, and it drew the eye, any-way, like a great mouth hungering for people to fall into it. It had an attraction about it, that frightened her, that added to her already considerable fears and discomforts one more dark anxiety.

Then she began to wonder, for it was a thing that seemed to possess a life of its own, that grew larger and larger, its growth not only keeping pace with the *Egret*, but outstripping it, racing ahead in a gigantic curve, as though endeavouring to cut across in front, as though possibly to encircle the *Egret* and swallow it up.

She didn't like to trouble Gerald, to worry him with the anxieties of a mere girl, because Gerald seemed so distant, so out of reach, but she *had* to tell him. Her hand went out and at that moment Gerald saw it for himself.

His mouth dropped open. His heart leapt. He almost didn't want to believe it just in case he was wrong. But he wasn't wrong. It was real. The cloud was coming to an end, at least in that part of the sky where the moon was. He'd be able to see to the ground!

Gerald started trembling and couldn't stop, for immediately he knew it was a mixed blessing. He had a chance now, however frail, but the responsibility of taking advantage of it was suddenly a great weight upon him. If the cloud had not broken he would have been free of blame. To be carried on to the end, helplessly, was not all bad.

Golly, what was he thinking? What was wrong with him?

How far ahead was it? Only a mile or two. In a minute he would be in the open and the wide world would be spread out beneath; dust or forest or mountains or plains.

'Oh my gosh,' he said, and glanced back.

He couldn't see the others, not really, just a feeling that heads and shoulders were all craning to one side. They had all seen. Everyone knew. Probably they were cheering or something like that. Lucky dogs. It was easy for them. They didn't know the half of it. They didn't know what it was like to be so terribly tired. They didn't know what it was like to long for the ground but to be so afraid of it. They would think the *Egret* was going down to safety.

They'd never know what hit them, but he'd know. He'd see it coming.

Suddenly the cloud was gone and there was a void, a pit; two vertical miles of nothing.

Gerald pushed the nose down into the emptiness and was almost sick with disbelief. There was the world shining in the light of the moon.

'It's the sea,' he cried.

What sea?

Or was it a lake?

Oh, golly; had that course set on the compass, 250 degrees, been the right one?

Was there a lake as large as this? Only salt lakes. Only dried-up salt lakes. There was none with water as large as this. There wasn't a lake in all Australia as large as this. The moonbeam was endless. It stretched away into evermore.

Oh, what a dirty trick. What a rotten, dirty trick. How could it be the sea? The wide open sea; wide open into the north, wide open into the east? What sea was it? The Tasman? The Coral Sea? The Arafura Sea? The Timor?

How silly could a fellow get? It couldn't be any of them. It must be a lake in flood. Lake Eyre, maybe. Could he have reached it? That'd be as big as this in flood. The drought had broken, hadn't it? Maybe there'd been a foot of rain in the last six hours. That would turn Lake Eyre from a desert of salt into an inland sea of tremendous size; maybe only a few inches deep, but a fellow would never see that from this height.

He heard the engine, suddenly becoming aware of it, winding up, over-riding the pitch. He was still going down, still diving, and the airspeed was up to 150 knots.

Oh, glory. So many things to think of. So many things not to forget.

He closed the throttle and edged the speed off and didn't know what to do next. What could a fellow do, except fly on, except wait? Keep the *Egret* in the air until the engine stopped and she *had* to go down?

Maybe it would be best to glide now, to conserve what fuel he had. From this height, with just a little power to keep the engine alive, he could glide for many miles. Perhaps that was the thing to do.

He set it for the glide, got the speed back to ninety knots, and the engine to a quiet burble. There was the horizon still to aid his balance, the faint leaden line of water and sky. And there was something else; an awareness of eyes, of five pairs of eyes, of five minds centred on him. He couldn't see them, couldn't hear their thoughts, but the reality of their presence was nerve-racking. He felt as though he stood alone on trial with eyes and questions shooting at him like arrows. He felt he wanted to shake a fist at them. What right did they have to judge him? But for him they'd all be dead. Who did they think they were?

Golly, a fellow was going round the bend. They wouldn't be thinking like that. They'd been marvellous all along. Still, that was easy enough for them, wasn't it? All they had to do was twiddle their thumbs, while he stared out in fear into a world of water. Though there was a line on it, on the starboard side. Something was there that didn't look like water. What the dickins was it? Could it be the shore? An island maybe? Or the desert fringe to the lake?

It was land. There was a line and a great shadow beyond it, a black, formless immensity.

By golly. There was no doubt about it. It was land all right. It must have been the lake in flood. He was in the centre of the continent!

For some reason or other he was immensely relieved. It

seemed so much better to be here than anywhere else. If he had gone over the edge of the continent into the ocean he'd never have found land. He'd have vanished, never to be heard of again. And who would search there, who would search the ocean for a little aeroplane that had disappeared in a dust storm in the north-west of New South Wales?

Lake Eyre. Oh, it was wonderful. For surely they would search here. Once they had worked out the winds and everything else that could have influenced the course of the *Egret*, the search planes would fan out in a great arc and they'd count Lake Eyre in and they would see the *Egret*. They couldn't miss her; a stark splash of colour in the unmarked desert, yellow and black and white. Sometimes he had thought the *Egret* looked horrible, that she stuck out like a sore thumb. And so she would. She'd be visible for miles. They'd find her.

He flew in towards the land, directly towards it, turning in, and he was down to about 6,000 feet, the engine still burbling, the wind still rushing.

It'd be easy to land on the desert. It'd be open and flat. He'd fly down until he could see the ground and gently reduce speed until he sank at just above forty knots. And then he'd sit there and wait and fly on and as soon as it touched switch off the engine. Then if anything went wrong, if he broke the undercarriage or turned over on his back, he wouldn't burn. If the engine was switched off the aircraft couldn't burn. Someone must have said that at some time. Even if he whacked down hard, even if they got bruised or broke a few limbs, they'd be all right, they wouldn't get killed, for in the desert there was nothing to hit, no trees or hills or great big rocks or fences or power-lines. All he had to do was to get the *Egret* on to the ground somehow and let Lady Luck do the rest.

He opened the engine to blow out the oil, the way his father did when he was gliding, then throttled back again, but gradually, in a vaguely uncomfortable way, found his attention riveting on the moonbeam, on that glimmering shaft of light lying across the water. It was curious. It wasn't smooth, as he had thought the lake would be. There were shadows in it. There was movement across it; and he had more than a suspicion that the movement and the shadows were waves, big waves, the sort that belonged to the sea.

Then he passed over the dark mass of the land and lost the moonbeam and began a wide, skidding turn to take him back across the water.

He was down to 5,000 feet.

When he crossed the shore again he looked back into the south, along the division between earth and water. Not that anything was plain to see, but it didn't look unlike the shores of a large lake in flood except for something that might have been a narrow strip of sand. There was a distinct but irregular line immediately adjoining the land, a change of colour. Three colours. Water, line and land.

It was the sea breaking on a beach.

Gerald shivered. It was as though he had stepped into a bitterly cold room. Did the others know? Unless they were blind they must have known. He had come to the sea and flown across it and reached land again. What sort of impossible joke was this? Or had he flown out into the great ocean and chanced upon an island?

Oh, glory. What sea was it? He was back to that unanswerable and incredible question. If this truly were the sea, he had flown with mighty winds behind him, winds of sixty, eighty, or a hundred miles an hour. So far from Coonabibba, that they might be lost for ever.

He was down to 3,000 feet and turning widely over the sea and the moonbeam was wheeling under the wing.

He gave the engine another burst to clear the oil, almost without thinking of it, and there was a misfire and a shower of sparks from the exhaust. It frightened him half out of his wits, but then the *Egret* purred on again, steadily.

What was the time? Seven-fifty-six. How long had he been up? Figures started beating him again. Must be getting on for seven hours – the absolute endurance of the *Egret*.

He had to go down. This time there was to be no continuing on course, no closing his eyes or his heart or his mind to the challenge of returning to the earth, no putting it off until later.

He was down to 2,300 feet now, flying parallel to the beach, heading south-west he thought, about half a mile offshore.

Where were the surface winds coming from? How strong were they? Should he land on the beach heading north or heading south? It was so hard to decide. Probably into the south would be best because he was almost certain that the winds higher up were blowing from that direction. It didn't go without saying that the winds on the surface were the same, but he had to make a decision one way or the other. All right, into the south, and perhaps the beach was curving that way.

He crept in more and continued to go down, then thought suddenly of something else.

He leant across to Jan and screamed, 'Safety belts! Tight!'

Jan's was tight already, but she twisted and looked back to the others and waved an arm. She couldn't see them very well, but they saw her, and understood. Bruce had made sure of it ages ago. For at least an hour all had sat crushed to their seats, each harness tightened until it could not be tightened more, so tight that they were numbed and bruised and tense with fear.

1,600 feet, about a quarter of a mile offshore, edging in, still going down, but the beach was narrow and its curves were tricky and it was all so difficult to see, to be sure. And he knew that flaps had to be used for landing, but how and in what way? It would be better not to try. He might end up wrecking everything. He should have practised when he was up above the clouds. He had decided to do it, made up his mind to it, then the thought had melted away. Oh, golly. All that time up there and he hadn't done it.

1,200 feet now on the altimeter, but it wasn't right. He was lower than that? The water looked so close. There were breakers to be seen, distinctly. A shaft of fear pierced him.

The altimeter was certainly wrong and he was 200 yards offshore.

Almost in panic he touched the rudder with his left foot, skidded the *Egret* over, pleaded for the land to rush out to meet him. And it did. The curving shore swept into his path, but the breakers, now on his right, didn't seem to be closer. He had lost 200 feet and they looked the same as before.

Ninety knots. Much, much too fast. How to get it back? How to stay on course? How to follow the beach? Its direction was so changeable.

Eighty knots, but now the controls felt funny. He had too much engine on, that was it. He was up and down and all over the place like a roller-coaster.

Engine off! It had to be done. And he did it numbly, in terror, and at once the engine note changed and he felt the seat drop from under him. Felt himself sinking into a world of *trees*.

In wildest alarm, he realized he had lost the beach. Sixty knots. Where was the beach? The controls were so sloppy and there was nothing but trees. Fifty knots. Nothing but trees. She was going, going to fall, going to drop clean out of the sky.

'Oh, God, please.' he screamed. 'God please. I don't know where I am, I can't see.'

But the speed was still fifty knots and still he floated. It felt like a leaf falling, like a leaf fluttering into an emptiness that might never come to an end.

'We'll be killed,' he screamed, and then the *Egret* struck and everything was black and shapeless and violent. There was a blow in his back like a swing from a club and a roaring sound in his head and suddenly he was in the air again, where he didn't know, how he didn't know, except that the nose was in the air again and the sky was swimming with watery stars and the bottom seemed to be falling out of a world that was breaking apart.

A thought crowded in somewhere that he had hit the beach after all, not the trees, hit the beach at the waterline, and that the *Egret* had bounced like a punctured rubber ball. He knew he had to switch off, but couldn't find the switch, not quickly enough. He fumbled wildly, but struck again in an eruption of spray.

The engine expired in a discharge of water and sound and sparks and the *Egret* twisted as though spinning on a roundabout, buckling into sand and water like some huge animal with failing legs.

Then there was quiet. Everything was quiet except for the sound of children crying.

9. Landfall

They were upright. At least they were not hanging upside down from their straps; but waves were breaking over the tail-plane and cracking against the side of the fuselage. There was water inside as well as outside, but Gerald couldn't move. He didn't know whether he was injured or not, but he knew he wanted to cry. The others were crying. Perhaps they started him off. A sob welled up and shook him and then another sob, and there wasn't any feeling of shame or embarrassment. Only exhaustion. Only a longing to sleep and to cry.

Someone came to him after a while and put a hand on his shoulder. He didn't know who it was and he didn't care and he didn't want to know. Then the hand went away.

It was Colin, dazed and weak, but conscious of the need to do something about escaping from the *Egret*. As far as he could see they were about fifteen yards offshore and there was pale moonlight and a beach and dark trees. He had a vague idea that it was very important to get away from a crashed aeroplane, but that the sea all around was going to make it awkward. Maybe if he opened the door the sea would flood in and they'd all drown before they could get out. Undecided, he stood there swaying, lost, even thinking about things that had no bearing on the situation at all. He had wanted to ask Gerald a question, but couldn't remember what it was.

The water was up to his knees, but it wasn't cold; cool at first, soothing, then almost warming. It seemed to take some of the ache away.

Then a voice said, 'Colin's not here. His seat's empty.' It was Carol.

'I'm here,' said Colin.

'Where?'

'Here.'

Bruce said rather tightly, 'Is every one all right?' There were one or two desultory answers and someone said, 'If we don't get out of here we'll drown.'

'I think I've broken something,' said Bruce. 'My leg's awful sore.'

Jan whimpered but didn't put anything into words. It was so hard to think with Gerald there beside her, shaking with almost soundless sobs. He was in an awful state. She wished he'd howl and get it over and done with.

'Probably you've only jarred your leg,' said Carol. 'You couldn't have broken it. It'd hurt terribly.'

'That's how it's hurtin'.'

Colin said, 'I reckon we could wade ashore all right. It's not that deep. About waist-high, I reckon.'

'The waves are rough.'

'Only because they're breaking.'

'What about my leg?'

'It can't be broken. No one else is hurt.'

'Who's going to be first to see if it's all right?' said Colin. 'No good me going. I can't swim with my clothes on.'

'I'll go,' said Jan.

'I reckon it ought to be a boy, not a girl.'

'I'm the best swimmer, aren't I? It ought to be me, even if I am a girl, or Bruce. Bruce can swim all right but not if he has a bad leg.'

'What I want to know is, where are we? What are we

doin' here?' Mark's voice was fretful.

'Oh, pipe down. We'll worry about that later.'

'Yeh; but what are we doin' in the sea? I mean t' say . . .'

Colin said, 'I think I'd better go first, Jan. After all, it's not right that a girl should go first.'

'But you said yourself that you can't swim with your clothes on.'

'I'll take them off.'

'Cor,' said Mark.

'It's *dark*, isn't it? It doesn't matter.'

'I'll tell.'

'Tell who?'

They almost heard his mouth open, but nothing came out. There wasn't anybody to tell. Even Mark knew that.

Colin peeled off to his underpants and said, 'All right, I'm going to open the door. Perhaps you'd all better stand up, in case the water comes in deep. Maybe you'd better help Gerald, Jan. I don't think he's very well.'

Jan didn't know what to do with Gerald, but didn't say anything, and Colin waded round Jim and tried to open the door. He couldn't shift it. He was still weak, but not so weak that a door was too much for him. He put his shoulder to it but it didn't give an inch.

'Crikey,' he said.

'What's wrong?'

'The blooming door won't open. Must be twisted or something.'

'Are you trying to open it inwards or outwards?'

'Outwards, of course. I'm not that silly.'

'Well, I suppose it's the weight of the sea against it.'

Imagine a girl thinking of that! Jan, of all people!

'I suppose you're right,' he said. 'Well, someone will have to give me a hand. We'll all have to get our shoulders against it and give a jolly good heave.'

'Can't you get out of the top of these things?' said Bruce. 'Don't they have a door in the roof? Give Gerald a dig in the ribs. Crikey, it's his aeroplane. He ought to know.'

'Gerald's sick,' said Colin.

'Fine time to get sick. Crikey, I've got a broken leg, but I'm carryin' on all right.'

'You're sure carrying on.'

'Shut up, Mark.'

Carol splashed past Colin and went to Gerald. Gerald meant a lot to her, and if he wasn't well she felt she had to be with him. When her hands closed on his shoulders she was astonished. He was shaking violently and though he tried to speak to her, he couldn't. His trembling was even in his throat and in his jaws. He couldn't control his tongue, but he made a noise and glanced to the clear panel of perspex behind his head. 'That's where you get out,' she said to Colin. 'It must be a door.'

Then she started smoothing Gerald's brow and his hair, stroking him gently with her fingers and whispering against his ear: 'It's all right. Everything's all right now. I'm so proud of you. Don't hold it in. Get rid of it.'

But Gerald couldn't. He hadn't been ashamed at the start, but he was now. He knew if he let go he'd scream and scream and scream and they'd wonder for ever afterwards what sort of boy he was. Somehow, with Carol, it might have been different, but not with the others. They'd never forget. They'd always hold it against him in their hearts. They'd forget all that he had done: they'd only remember that afterwards he had screamed. He was a Hennessy. Hennessys didn't do that sort of thing.

Colin went out through the roof and slid over the side into the water, dropping immediately to chest depth. In surges it was up to his chin. They'd have to swim for it, particularly the shorter ones, and there was an undertow to be reckoned with, too. It even crushed him against the side of the aircraft as the waves went out, threatening to drag him down. It alarmed Colin, because he wasn't used to the sea; his swimming had been done in pools and billabongs and the backwaters of rivers.

Jan appeared above him, squatting on the wing. 'What's it like?' she said.

'No good. It's dangerous.'

'We'll have to get out,' Jan said, 'because she's shifting. She shifted just now. She's gone over on one side.'

'The aeroplane has?'

'That's right.'

'Crumbs. Mark will drown for sure. He can't swim for nuts. And I don't think I could hold him. He gets so panicky in water.'

'He doesn't seem to be panicky. He seems to have more cheek than anyone.'

'That's because he can't see what's out here . . . I wonder whether there's a rope or anything? We could tie it to something here then I could run it ashore. Because there's Bruce, too. If anything's really wrong with his leg . . .'

'Bruce is a great big baby.'

'Yeh; but just the same . . . something must be wrong with it.'

'I'll see if I can find a rope.'

Jan disappeared and Colin locked his fingers round the wing strut and hung on, swaying to the surges of the sea. He could hear the waves breaking on the shore and the huge, continuous murmur that was the restless sea itself. He could distinguish more now, too. Detail after detail of his surroundings registered on his mind, one after the other, like a sum that he was adding up. From the attitude of the *Egret* he knew the undercarriage was snapped off, the tail-plane broken, and the propeller bent almost like a soft candle. He could see huge boulders along the beach, massive outcrops of rock, which somehow the plunging and skidding *Egret* had managed to avoid. He could see shore-line trees, spindly, twisted things tossing in gusts of wind, and he could see in the sky signs of unmistakable and deepening gloom in the south. But no lights. Nowhere a light, nowhere a glimmer that might have betrayed the presence of human habitation. It was far too early for people to have gone to bed. This was a deserted coast. Where had Gerald brought them? Did Gerald know? Was he in that state because he knew or because he didn't know?

'I've got a rope!'

It was Jan, up above him again, looking down from the wing.

'Oh good. That's great.'

'There's a tomahawk, too, and a little spade. Bruce says it's the crash kit. Do you want them?'

'Just give me the rope for now, but don't lose the other things, will you?'

'No fear.'

'I hope the rope's long enough. Do you think it is?'

'I don't know.'

Jan passed it down, still coiled up, still knotted in its coil. Dumb girl. She should have untied it for him. He struggled with it and said, 'Get everything together, Jan. All our suitcases and things and everything that you can find. And if there's a map, for Pete's sake bring it.'

The knot came undone and the coil fell apart in his hands. He was scared it was going to tangle.

'Is that all you want me to do?' said Jan.

'Just get everything together and out on the wing. Go on, go on. Get moving. It's not a blooming picnic.'

'All right! Keep your hair on. What about Mr Jim?'

'What about him? What can we possibly do about him? Go on, Jan. Do as I say. *Please!*'

He got the end of the rope tied round the strut, but the rope wasn't easy to handle in the dark, or in the water, then he started off for the shore, sometimes on his feet,

sometimes swimming, sometimes even dragged under by the current. The rope was an awful handicap; he kept getting his legs caught in it and he was afraid he was going to lose hold of the end. If only he didn't feel so weak. He knew that if he lost the rope, it'd get tangled round the aircraft and then what would he do? But suddenly he was scrambling up the shelving sand and the sea was running back behind him and there were still yards of rope to go, enough rope to carry it to a boulder, run it twice round the circumference and knot it. Oh, for once things were going right. Was it secure? Yes, it was. It'd hold a horse.

He ran back to the water's edge and already two or three figures were up on the wing and it looked like another struggling up through the hatch. One, two, three, four. Four there were. Who was still below? Bruce with a broken leg or Gerald in too much of a fizz to help himself?

'Come on,' Colin bellowed, 'get moving off there!'

He waded out, hand over hand, along the rope, and two people slid off the edge of the aircraft, one shrieking at the top of his voice. It was Mark, performing like something out of a circus. Obviously he hadn't slid off, he'd been pushed. 'Clock him one,' bellowed Colin. 'Knock him on the head.'

There was a wild struggle going on in the water, Mark gurgling and screaming and Jan shouting, but Colin got there and grabbed his brother by the hair of his head and roared at him. 'Shut up, you little fool! You're all right. You're not going to drown.'

Mark was way past understanding, because when the sea surged he was out of his depth and couldn't put his feet down and his eyes and mouth and nose were full of water and his only instinct was to fight. Colin didn't know what to do with him, except bang his head against the wing strut, as hard as he could bang it, even though the effort cost him his own foothold. They both went under and by the time Colin got up for air he had taken two great swallows of the sea. He spluttered and clawed his hair out of his eyes, but Jan was there to steady him and put his free hand on the rope.

'Have you got him?' Jan cried.

'Yeh, yeh. I'm right. I'll take him. Stupid little so-and-so.'

From up on top Bruce edged down into the heaving water, hanging grimly by one hand to Carol's lengthening arm, his fingers fastened to her wrist like a vice, in complete dependence upon her. His right leg was so sore below the knee that it affected his use of the rest of his body. If it hadn't been for Carol and Mark he would never have got up through the escape hatch. He had almost cried from the pain; they'd been pretty rough with him. He was an awful weight for the straining girl to bear, a solid lump. Though Carol looked almost a young woman, she had only the strength of a child. 'Let go,' she pleaded with him, 'please let go, Bruce. You're too heavy. I'm slipping.' But he wouldn't let go and dragged her down after him, shrieking. It might have ended in tragedy, but Carol could swim well enough to save her life and the water gave Bruce a mobility he had not had before. But it did mean that no one was left behind to urge Gerald on or to pass down the suitcases and the bits and pieces they had salvaged from the aircraft. The three of them, Jan, Carol, and Bruce, clung to the rope, abusing each other. For about the first time ever Carol didn't sound like a lady.

Colin, by then, had struggled to the shore with Mark, dragged him up the sand and dumped him on his face above the water line. He felt so mad with Mark he could cheerfully have kicked him, but all he had left was enough energy to flop on the sand, prop himself up by one elbow, and pant for breath. How often had he tried to get Mark to learn how to swim? But Mark *wouldn't*. He was so stubborn about it, and for no reason at all, except that water made him cold!

Mark was all right; he had a fair load of sea-water on board; but he could groan, he could mumble, he could moan about the pain in his head. Mark would survive. But the others, blow them, were awful slow getting away.

Colin reeled down in the shallows and saw Jan coming in along the rope with Bruce, pulling him behind her like a toy boat on a string. Carol, unless he was mistaken, was still out beside the *Egret*, banging a fist on the fuselage and shouting for Gerald.

'Give us a hand,' wailed Jan. 'There's something wrong with his leg all right. At least, if there isn't, I'll kill him.

'What's happening out there?' said Colin.

'Oh, this big drip pulled Carol in. It's all his fault. Give us a hand, Col. I'll never get him up the beach; he can't walk.'

'Is Gerald still inside?'

'From the noise that Carol's making he must be . . . hey, hey! Come back. Give us a hand.'

'He'll walk if he's got to.'

'Fair go, Col,' said Bruce. 'Give her a hand. I can't put my leg down. Fair dinkum, I can't.'

Colin took no notice of them. He was already half-way to the *Egret* shouting at Carol, 'What's wrong out there? What's wrong with Gerald? Why won't he come?'

He reached Carol. She was still beating on the side of the fuselage, screaming Gerald's name. Only her head was above water and Colin knew she had already been under once or twice. There was no doubt that the tide was coming in. All that it needed to swamp the *Egret* was a breaker in the wrong place.

'Leave Gerald to me,' he yelled, 'you get to the beach.'

'Gerald . . .' she whimpered.

'He'll be all right. He's probably only getting the stuff together.'

'The stuff's up on top already. It's all there waiting. That stupid Bruce; he pulled me in. Why doesn't Gerald answer?'

'Will you stop worrying about Gerald and get yourself up on to that beach!'

'Don't you talk to me like that!'

'I'll talk to you any way I please. Do you want to drown or something, you silly dope? The tide's coming in. Get moving!'

She seemed to hiss at him through her teeth. He couldn't see her face but was sure there was hatred all over it, a fierceness that he couldn't understand. Suddenly, he was so mad with her that he swore at her, then swam to the tail of the *Egret* and dragged himself up on to it irritably and scrambled along the fuselage until he came to the escape hatch. The suitcases were there and lots of odds and ends, but no sign of Gerald.

He dropped down inside almost before he realized that he had done it. He wasn't being brave; it was sheer impulse and the carry-over from his row with Carol. He was angry because he had sworn at her. Colin hardly ever swore. He was dwelling more on that than anything else until he discovered how much the *Egret* had shifted – or how high the tide had risen. Water was lapping at his chest and all sorts of things were floating around.

'Gerald,' he yelled in sudden fright. 'Where are you?'

Gerald was there all right, still more or less in his seat, with his head against the side of the aircraft, water up to his chin. Colin couldn't see him, but he found him with his hands, and recoiled from him, horrified. He was sure Gerald was dead. He felt like something dead, like a poor dead animal, drowned.

'Gerald,' he cried, then felt the *Egret* lurch again, felt it slip on the seabed, felt a rain of spray from the hatch and the wildest spasm of alarm for his own safety. He was trapped; he was nailed in. It was madness. What on earth was he doing here? How had he come to be here? In that instant he wanted only to claw up through the hatch and swim for his life. But a completely unwanted sense of obligation drove his hands to feel for Gerald again, and when he found him the shock was like a punch. It was like the dead coming to life or the sleeping to violent consciousness. Gerald was under water, right under, but he was struggling and his fingers found Colin's arms and almost dragged him down. It was like a nightmare.

Colin found himself heaving and pulling and wrenching at Gerald to break the curious hold that the seat seemed to have on him. It was part of the same fight; it was Gerald's life or his, or their two lives together. They fought but Gerald couldn't break free. He was still strapped in!

Colin panicked and a rush of thoughts that were wholly bad almost consumed him. It would have been better if Gerald had been dead. Then he could have got out himself. Then there would have been nothing to stop him. 'He's dead, Carol. There was nothing I could do.' But she wouldn't believe him; she'd have felt the *Egret* lurch; she was outside banging on its outer skin. She'd know that the lurch had frightened him. She'd tell. Then everyone would know that Colin had left his mate to die.

Oh, it was an awful instant, crowded with horror and with the violence of his savage and desperate thrust that broke Gerald's grip; horror and violence and then wild elation when he knew that Gerald had let go. He could escape. He could get out and no one would ever know. How could they ever really know if he never told them?

But that way of thinking wasn't his own way of thinking; it was something evil that was trying to destroy perhaps both of them; an alien instant when his mind, like an explosion, rushed in all directions at once, but when his body, suddenly freed, elected to drive on downwards to the clasp of the seat harness in Gerald's lap.

Gerald burst out, burst upwards, and the two boys fell into a floundering heap of limbs under water. There were all sorts of things in that water, limbs that didn't belong to them, clothing, seats, sharp edges. Colin broke through for air, then managed to find Gerald's head and shoulders and dragged them above the surface. But the hatchway was still above him; it wasn't a door that he could walk through, pulling Gerald after him. How could he go *up*? They'd never get out, not the two of them.

Carol screamed, 'Lift him up! Come on! Lift him up!'

Her head was there, showing faintly against that square of moon-grey sky and her arms were reaching down. It wasn't far, not really. The *Egret* wasn't as big as a house, the hatch wasn't yards above them. A tall man had to stoop in her; even a boy sometimes felt the need to duck.

'Help me, Gerald.' But Gerald couldn't. His knees were like broken reeds. Colin heaved him upright, reeling and staggering, and Carol caught him by the head and edged her hands under his armpits.

'Heave,' she said.

Colin heaved and the pain of the effort was like an incision in his back.

'Again.'

He heaved again, he pushed, he strained until he thought that something would snap, and suddenly the weight was gone, there was a frantic scuffling overhead and a heavy splash. They were overboard.

Colin almost cried from his weariness, but he clawed up through the hatch and saw them both in the water on the shoreward side, not far from where the rope would have been. Carol was splashing round and shouting for help, and someone, probably Jan, was already wading out.

Everything was all right. He wouldn't have to do any more.

Colin sighed. Perhaps it was a groan more than a sigh, of relief and disbelief and bone tiredness. He squatted near the hatch, clinging to the lip of it, waiting until Jan had taken charge and the others in the water were out of danger.

Then he saw something else in the water; debris, things floating and swirling, half-sunken things, bits of paper, a shirt. His groan of relief and tiredness ran into a groan of dismay.

It was their luggage. The incoming waves had broken over all their things and swept them from the wing into the sea. He'd never be able to get them. Not in a lifetime.

Colin slid over the side and made his way ashore along the rope, hand over hand, his feet often off the bottom.

Gerald had a lot of water in him and Jan attended to him. She stretched him out on the sand, knelt beside him, and started pumping his arms and squeezing her hands into the small of his back as she had been taught to do, while Carol looked on fearfully and wretchedly, vaguely bitter inside because Jan was doing it and she wasn't. Jan knew how to do it and she didn't.

Jan did it just as she had done it at the pool, practising on her friends under the eye of her swimming teacher. But no one's life had depended upon it before and she didn't really know if it would work. Then the water came up. It worked all right. And soon she had Gerald breathing regularly. Then he rolled on his side, almost of his own accord, and started mumbling and Carol said, 'Oh, thanks, Jan. Thanks, Jan. Thanks Jan.'

Jan sat back on her heels, panting, aching from the force she had applied, trying to put Carol's words together.

They were like drumbeats in the distance, full of meaning to other people but without a message for her.

Colin flopped down nearby, his skin pale and wet and glistening in the moonlight, his thin body shaking from fatigue. He, too, was mumbling: 'What am I gonna wear? I haven't got any clothes. I've lost m'best suit. Me Mum'll scalp me.'

Mark came and sat beside him but couldn't understand what his brother was saying. It was just a murmur, a moaning sound.

'My head's sore,' said Mark. 'You belted me. You hit me, you did. When I tell Dad he'll give you a hidin'.'

Colin mumbled on, not hearing him, lost in his own sorrow. Colin was always so well turned out. Losing his clothes was a real tragedy for Colin.

Bruce nursed his leg. He felt it up and down again and again like someone mesmerized, like someone ordered to repeat a single act. He was sure it was broken, but Jan said it wasn't. It hurt like crazy, but no one cared, no one was interested. He felt over it with the flat of his hand and with his fingertips, sure that he would find, sooner or later, a sharp piece of bone breaking the skin. But there weren't any breaks or bends or blood, and it was too dark to look for bruises. No one cared. And the mosquitoes were a blooming pest. They had teeth like tigers, the blooming things. And he was so hungry. He could eat an ox, horns and all. And he was so tired; so tired and sore and hungry and itching and sick of everything. It was like something out of one of Jan's dreams.

He stretched out his leg, painfully and slowly, put his head down, closed his eyes and went to sleep.

Colin went to sleep, too, and Gerald didn't really wake up. Jan slipped over on her side in a tight little ball and knew nothing about it, and soon Carol too ceased to be aware of her surroundings. Mark was left on his own, sitting up, holding his throbbing head. But he didn't know that the others had left him on his own, for little by little the ache became a numbness and soon he did not hear even the thud of the waves on the shore.

10. Nowhere

There was light and greyness and the clean smell of the morning and the sound of waves drumming softly.

Mark knew what it was all about. The instant he awoke he knew it was sand that he had slept on and that the birds he could hear were gulls. Everything was remembered; nothing was forgotten; not even his terror when they had pushed him into the water, not even Colin's brutal hand banging his head against the strut.

He sat up, creaking a little in his bones, numb in his flesh. He was rather cold and a bit shivery. His clothes were still wet and gritty, but his head felt better. He felt for the lump that had been there the night before but it had gone. So had the sharp, throbbing pain. So, too, had the *Egret*.

His eyes ran down the long shelf of sand to where he was sure the *Egret* had been. All that was left was a frayed and broken rope lying like a tattered reptile at the foot of a boulder.

He lurched to his feet to view this astonishing thing more clearly. Colin and the others were still sprawled on the sand in all sorts of extraordinary attitudes, still asleep, all of them, and the tide had run out a long way and the sun wasn't up and the sky was heavily overcast. It wasn't daylight, it was an in-between light, as though the day had opened a door but had not yet stepped in.

Where was the *Egret*?

Something was there. He could see it better now; a dark mass like a rock and along the beach there were more dark masses like rocks or slabs of stone. Perhaps they were stones. Perhaps they were wreckage.

It was wreckage all right. The *Egret* was smashed to bits. There were bits of it everywhere half-buried in sand, great lumps of it in a ragged line around the curve of the beach. Surely they hadn't slept through a storm? Perhaps they had, because Mark suddenly felt full of sand and

when he looked closer at the others they were covered in
sand, dusted with it. Colin looked like a figure of a sleeping boy hewn out of sandstone.

Surely they hadn't slept through a storm?

Mark brushed the sand off himself, spat it from his
mouth and shook it from his hair, then took off his shoes
and socks and walked down to where the *Egret* had been.
It was the engine that was there and the propeller and a
tangle of wires and cables and pipes, all ragged and broken
as though a sea monster had bitten it off. Thick, slow oil
was still bleeding from it and dripping into the sand.
What a shame. That beaut little aeroplane all chewed to
bits.

It was a funny feeling, standing there, with his toes
slowly sinking and curling into the sand, and the greyness
round about, the smell of the sea, and the sound of the
sea, and the silence that was there, too. Strange the way
the feeling came creeping up on him, almost as though he
had become a balloon floating in an empty and aching
place; like being completely alone and light-headed; like
still being asleep, perhaps; like not being Mark Kerr any
more, but someone different that he wasn't even sure that
he knew very well, because the eagerness that he usually
felt first thing every morning to get the day rolling, to get
it started, to leap about for the sheer joy of living, just
wasn't there. Instead, there was a flatness, a greyness.

Everything familiar seemed to have gone a long way
away and Mark didn't like it very much. He liked a bit of
friendly noise in the morning, the wireless going and
screen doors slamming and hens squawking down the yard
and dogs barking and the clatter of milk bottles and men's
voices from the dairy depot across the road. He liked the
world to be alive and kicking. He didn't like churches or
the silent minute on Anzac Day. He didn't like hospitals

or rubbish tips or places where people were quiet or in pain.

He didn't much like standing near the aeroplane, either, with that thick, slow oil bleeding from it and dripping into the sand, even though there were things lying round that were as good as pirates' treasure; interesting looking bits of aeroplane, metal tabs with important printing on, and instruments worth lots and lots of money. If a fella owned an instrument like one of these his mates would come from miles and miles around to have a look at it, but maybe Gerald wouldn't like it if he took one. Or that blooming old Carol either. They'd call him a thief, probably, and take it off him. Maybe Bruce would, too, because Bruce hadn't been very nice to him either.

Mark looked up the beach to where they were lying; still sprawling there, all of them. Fancy not waking up. But it was the same at home. No one woke up there either until the day was half done.

Mark scowled at them and would have gone up and yelled 'Wakey, wakey,' except that he had lost confidence. His skin was pretty thick, but not so thick that their impatience and crossness with him had failed to get through. But Colin was different, of course. Colin was his brother. Colin knocked him about more than anyone, but Colin was different just the same. A fella could take from his family things he would never take from anyone else. Yeh; but he didn't want to go, somehow, not even to Colin.

He mooched off along the sand, digging his toes in, taking a meandering path from stone to stone, from shell to shell, even from one bit of wreckage to another, sometimes scratching himself, sometimes belching magnificently. (At school his belch was famous.) He had a very empty tummy and it rumbled and bubbled and he got to thinking about breakfast and eyed off a couple of cheeky-looking seagulls. Maybe a seagull cooking on the spit would make some sort of a beginning to the day!

He tried to run one down, but it took off and flew away. He tried aiming rocks at others but their flight was too nimble. So he called them a few names and pulled on his hair in irritation, an unconscious mannerism borrowed from his mother, and looked back to where the *Egret* was. No one was sitting up; no one was awake; or at least he didn't think so. The light wasn't good, but not so bad that a fella couldn't see a few hundred yards.

He trudged on a bit farther, farther away from them, then stopped quite suddenly, quite breathlessly.

Mark didn't actually feel sick, but almost. There was a heavy thud of his heart that seemed to strike at his insides from all directions.

There was something on the sand, up near the high tide mark, up there where shell fragments and seaweed looked like a grease ring round a bath.

'Gee,' he said, in a tiny voice, and started backing away, started going weak at the knees.

It was a body. It was Mr Jim.

Then he stumbled and sat down heavily, backwards, and pressed the palms of his hands into his eyes and felt awfully cold and not at all hungry any more.

'Oh, gee,' he said, and started shivering, but not thinking about anything very much, not even about Mr Jim.

After a while he got up on to his feet and headed towards the *Egret*, not absolutely certain that he hadn't imagined it, but not brave enough to go back to make sure. Perhaps it wasn't Mr Jim, anyway. Perhaps it was Gerald or Bruce. Perhaps one of them had wandered off and gone to sleep farther up the beach? He hadn't taken *that* much notice of them when he'd woken up.

But they were all there. When he got back they were all

there; all like *dead* people, the lot of them. They weren't dead, of course. They couldn't be! They wouldn't dare die on him!

He dropped beside Colin and shook him by the shoulder, and it took a dismaying length of time for Colin's eyes to open. Colin turned his head then, though not the rest of his body, and met the quite extraordinary relief in Mark's young face. But nothing much registered with Colin, not for a moment or two. Then he turned over and sat up slowly, pushing himself up on an arm. 'Morning, is it?' he groaned. And said nothing more, for there was dried blood caked with sand on his thigh and across his midriff.

Mark saw it, too. 'You're *hurt*!' he squealed.

Colin flinched from fright because it did look awful.

'Does it hurt, Col?'

No; it didn't hurt. Felt a bit peculiar, but it didn't hurt. He'd had a lump of chewing gum stuck hard to his leg once; it felt something like that.

'Does it hurt?' repeated Mark.

'No. But I don't remember anything about it . . .' Colin pressed his fingers round the bloodstains. 'Seems to be all right, though,' he said. 'I must have cut myself somewhere.' Then he looked down the beach and saw that the *Egret* wasn't there. 'Crikey,' he exclaimed. 'Where's it gone?'

'Smashed to pieces.'

'It isn't!'

'It is,' said Mark, full of importance. 'You come and look. You come and see for yourself.'

'Crikey . . .'

'Say, Col . . . How are we going to get away again?'

Colin squinted at his brother. 'You *didn't* think he'd fly it off again, did you?'

From the look of Mark it seemed that he might have done.

'For cryin' out loud. Fly it off again? It was a wreck last night, nip, even *before* this happened. We *crashed,* or didn't you know?'

Mark looked crestfallen and Colin got to his feet, his skin twitching to the irritation of the sand. He brushed it slowly away as though it was an effort to concentrate on any form of labour. He'd felt all right sitting down, but weak and horribly empty now that he was standing up. His stomach was so flat it curved inwards. Then he stretched himself and ran the palms of his hands across his ribs – Colin's ribs stuck out, particularly when he breathed in – and looked at his watch, then held it to his ear and shook his wrist and held it to his ear again. 'Oh, blow,' he said. 'Water in it, I suppose. What time do you reckon it is?'

'I don't know.' Mark was eager to be off. There were bits of the aeroplane that he thought he'd like to save and he wanted to get in first. With Colin beside him it would be all right to pick things up. 'Coming down to have a look?' Mark urged.

'Sun's up,' said Colin, 'but you wouldn't think so, would you? Fancy finding ourselves at the beach. Haven't been to the beach for ages.'

Mark had been only twice in his life and the first time he'd been too young to remember it. 'Come on, come on. Don't you want to have a look at the aeroplane?'

'What aeroplane?'

'There are bits of it.'

Then for some reason he couldn't explain (perhaps one of the girls moved) Colin was suddenly and acutely aware of his underpants. In an instant he felt furtive and flustered and extremely uncomfortable. Suddenly, everything else was forgotten. 'What am I going to wear?' he wailed.

'Eh?' said Mark. He hadn't really noticed anything amiss.

'I haven't got any *clothes*.'

'Swipe me,' said Mark, 'neither you have.'

It had been Carol who had moved, for now she threw out an arm and rolled over and groaned like someone in pain. Colin didn't wait for anything else. He bolted. He ran this way and that like a startled rabbit, and finally into the cover of the foreshore trees. And when he got there he stood behind a tree trunk hugging himself, panting and trembling and wondering what on earth he was going to do. It wasn't as if he had been caught by surprise and could duck into his bedroom and pull on a pair of jeans, or that the other fellows had anything to give him either.

'Aw, crikey,' he shuddered. 'It's the real end.'

Mark trailed in after him, scratching his disordered hair. The sand was getting on his nerves. 'You're decent, you know,' he said. 'Honest you are. I'd say if you weren't.'

'I'm not,' said Colin sullenly. 'It's the sort of thing that *would* happen to me.' Mark wondered then whether he should say something about Mr Jim, but if he said anything they'd have to act on it and that was an awful thought. If he kept his mouth shut the problem might go away somewhere.

Carol was surprised when she sat up, for in effect she was alone. She thought she'd heard voices but there was no one, only three sleeping figures and the clearly defined tracks of footprints in the sand.

She felt awfully depressed; there was a blackness inside her and a nagging sense of foreboding, of disaster. It was such a desolate and silent beach. Waves were thudding and birds were crying, but they added to the silence; they took nothing away from it.

She drew her knees up under her chin and felt a perfect mess. And she was cold and hungry and sticky and afraid. Where were they? Where had Gerald brought them? He'd been flying to Coonabibba, not to the sea. Because it was the sea; it was the ocean that lay out there, grey and gloomy and sombre and enormous. And the shoreline was so forbidding; leggy, twisted trees with dark, dirty green leaves, and rock outcrops, and rubbish that looked like the spoils of a storm strewn along the sand.

It was Gerald's birthday. The thought saddened her even more. She turned her head to him. He was asleep. He still looked exhausted and so awfully young, like a little boy. She reached out a hand to him but didn't touch him, dropped her hand in the sand near his face and said, 'Oh, Gerald . . . We're all going to die. We've got nothing to eat. Where have you brought us, Gerald?'

Jan said, 'Hi.'

Carol turned sharply, guiltily. Jan's clouded eyes were looking at her.

'Hi,' Carol said, after a pause. (What was Jan thinking?)

'Do you really think it's that bad, Carol?'

'Well, where are we?' Though it wasn't really a question.

'I don't know. Looks like a desert island to me. But how could it be?'

'There's been a storm. Even the aeroplane's gone.'

'Yeh . . . Yeh; it's not the sort of thing you'd expect, is it? Do you think we'd better see if anything's been washed up? We might find some of our things.'

'I suppose that's where Mark and Colin have gone . . . I'm hungry, Jan. Are you?'

'Starving.'

Jan shivered on to her feet and brushed the sand from her clothes and wriggled uncomfortably. There was more sand in her clothes than on them. 'Cold, isn't it? Perhaps we've gone south, Carol.'

'It's very early. There's no sun, you know.'

'Hasn't rained though.'

'Would we know if it had?'

Jan kicked her shoes off vigorously and flexed her toes. 'Come on, let's see if we can find anything. Once the tide starts coming in again we'll lose it all.'

'I'll tell you what we will find.'

'What's that?'

Carol choked on it. 'A body.'

Jan froze. It was awful. She'd forgotten about poor Mr Jim. After a while she sat down again and turned her head away and started crying softly. She couldn't face the thought of finding poor Mr Jim.

Mark edged down behind them and stood a short way off waiting for them to see him. If it had been only Jan who was awake he wouldn't have cared, but he was frightened of Carol. In fact, many things were beginning to frighten Mark more and more. All sorts of vague fears about the sea being there and the *Egret* not being there, about the absence of familiar things, about Mr Jim, about the unspeakable gulf that seemed to yawn between him and his parents. Even Colin's pants. What sort of a joke was it when a fella didn't have a pair of pants to wear? And didn't look like getting any, either.

He waited for the girls to turn round but they didn't and he felt awkward, wondering what to do with himself. A fella felt a complete nut standing there. He edged closer and said, 'I say . . .'

But they didn't hear him because the breeze was coming in off the sea, so he went towards them dancing on his toes to make out that he had just come in from a run along the beach. 'Hi, there,' he called. 'What's cookin'?' He should have done that in the first place, but it wasn't easy with Carol being there.

'Hello,' said Carol. 'Where's Colin?'

'Around,' said Mark with a shrug, and dropped a few feet from Jan, but she turned her head away. He didn't know she was crying and thought that she, too, had developed a hate on him. He felt more unwanted than ever. So the things he had wanted to say about Colin's pants were not said. Even the things he might have said about Mr Jim were not said either. He grew silent and miserable and drew sad little circles in the sand with his fingers.

After a while Jan asked, 'What was that about Colin?'

Mark turned his head slowly in her direction but didn't really look at her, because that was where Mr Jim was, up that way, behind her. 'He's around,' he said.

'Around where?'

'Oh, somewhere. I don't know.'

'He hasn't salvaged anything, then?'

'Eh?'

'Salvaged anything! Picked things up! Gone looking for things?'

'No . . .'

'What's wrong with you?' She sounded irritable and unfriendly.

'Nothin',' he said, and got up and walked away and sat on his own, turning his back on them. He felt so glum that a great big tear dribbled down his cheek. He had a jolly good mind to tell them about Mr Jim, just to make them unhappy, too.

'Golly,' said Bruce. 'Just look at my ankle. I knew I'd done something.'

'So you're awake!' said Jan. 'About time.'

'I told you I'd broken it. Look at it. Black and blue.'

'It's bruised, that's all, or sprained or something.'

'Strike me pink!' roared Bruce. *'Where's the Egret?'*

Gerald sat up sharply, almost as though prodded with a pin, then fell back giddily, his head swimming, his stomach turning over, and instantly Carol was at him, like a hen with a chick, fussing. 'Oh, go away,' he said and struggled up again, this time on his hands and knees.

'The *Egret's* gone, Gerald,' Bruce shrieked and Mark ran over, his tears forgotten, because the boys were awake and if they wanted to know anything about the *Egret*, he knew the lot. 'Yeh, yeh,' he cried, 'all in bits. Smashed to bits. I've seen it. I've been down to look. Come on, come on, I'll show you.'

Gerald moaned. It was quite frightening, because he was down on all fours and his eyes had widened and his teeth were showing. It was so startling that when it happened it was immediately more important than anything else. Then Gerald scrambled away down the beach for five or six yards on his knees before he managed to flounder to his feet.

'He's flipped!' Bruce cried. He tried to get up, tried to follow Gerald because he was running towards the sea, but his leg gave way with an excruciating twist of pain. It was Carol who went after Gerald, and then Mark; Mark not in too much of a hurry because Mark was a very frightened little boy. In fact he went only a short distance then looked back, appealing with his hands for Bruce's support, but Bruce had to be counted out. Mark screamed, 'Colin! Colin! Colin!' And then ran back up the beach to where he had left his brother in hiding.

'This blooming leg,' Bruce shrieked and turned on his thunderstruck sister. 'Go after them, you dumb Dora.'

Carol caught up with Gerald down where the engine was lying, though what she'd do if he turned on her she didn't have the faintest idea. She was almost sick with unbelief, almost sure in her heart that Bruce was right; and she was panicking inside, emptying inside, for she had no understanding of this sort of thing. It was part of the world that was hidden from people. But when Gerald realized that she had come up behind him, he changed. His mood fell away, seemed to peel off him like a disguise reluctantly shed.

But he said nothing and when she touched him he held on to her hand, squeezed it for two or three seconds, then let go. After a while, he said, rather strangely, 'So what?

It was insured.' Then suddenly sobbed: 'It was a lovely little aeroplane. It worked so hard for me. It's not fair.'

By then Jan was there, but standing back, all muddled up, embarrassed, turning her big toe into the sand, and Bruce was surer than ever that his leg really was broken, and Colin had come to the edge of the trees with Mark.

'What's all the fuss about?' said Colin. 'You said Gerald had gone off his nut. I reckon you're the nut.'

'I'm not, you know,' declared Mark with heat. 'Even Bruce said so and every one was runnin' in circles. I thought he was goin' to run into the sea and drown himself.'

'I reckon you ought to run into the sea and drown yourself.'

'Come on back with me, Col. Don't hide any more.'

'I want some pants first.'

'Oh *blow*,' said Mark and pouted. 'Well, I'm not goin' back either. I don't like 'em. They're all nasty to me.'

Jan wasn't sure whether or not she should drift out of the picture. She always felt like something tacked on when Gerald and Carol were together, but this was different, because Gerald wasn't well. (Colin had said that hours ago, hadn't he? Perhaps Colin had been a jump ahead of the lot of them?)

Gerald was so peculiar; he'd been peculiar in the aeroplane. Perhaps something had happened to him, *snapped*, perhaps. That was the word that grown-ups used. She'd heard before of people doing odd things after they had been through a terrible ordeal. Was that why he had flown on and on and acted so strangely at times? She'd watched him from the corner of her eye in the aeroplane; she'd seen his long periods of intense agitation, his fast-changing moods, she'd seen him talking to himself, she'd seen his wide-eyed horror though she'd tried not to look, just as she had seen it again this morning.

Jan tried to grapple with the thought, but it was hard. More the sort of thing that grown-ups would know how to handle. When grown-ups started talking about things that disturbed the mind they always sent children out of the room. Was it possible that Gerald's mind was disturbed? Was this what people meant by that phrase?

How were they going to handle Gerald if he turned violent? Bruce was the only one strong enough (Colin was such a weed; so thin) but Bruce had been hurt. She felt guilty about Bruce because she had called him a big baby; but it was Gerald who was the baby; Bruce was the one who was really hurt.

Jan went back to him and said, 'Gerald's all right; I I think.'

Bruce grimaced. Anyone with two sound legs must be all right. He was beginning to feel very sorry for himself.

'I'll take a look at it again, if you like,' Jan said.

'Arrgh. What good'll that do? You don't care.'

'If you're hurt of course I care. I thought you were putting it on.'

'Putting it on! And it's black and blue!'

'Well, you always make the most of everything.'

Bruce scowled and Jan bent towards him. 'You hurt me, sis,' he said, 'and I'll crown you.'

'Well, let me look at it!'

'What are you going to do? Put it in splints or some thing? You'll make it worse. If you really cared you'd go for a doctor.'

She dropped back from him. 'Be fair, Bruce. Where are we going to find a doctor?'

'How do I know? And how do *you* know until you look? There could be a town back there for all we know.'

'You know very well there isn't.'

'I don't know any such thing. Just because there's no one round here doesn't mean there's no one around anywhere. Who'd be down at the beach at this hour, anyway, on a morning like this, cold as bloomin' charity?'

It was a point. It really was. There could have been a town back there, maybe half a mile, or a mile, or five miles away. There might have been a town round the next headland, the headland on the left or the headland on the right.

Bruce could see that he had made his point; not that he had thought of it until he had said it. 'Well?'

'I suppose you're right,' Jan said, 'and you're not the only reason either, are you?'

'You mean Gerald?'

'I mean Mum and Dad and everyone. They'll be frantic. They'll think we're dead . . .'

That was what Carol wanted to say to Gerald, too; that they should be up and moving, doing something, going somewhere; but Gerald still seemed to be two people, his real self and a stranger. Carol could sense it and Gerald was convinced of it.

The stranger seemed to be running round inside him in a panic, as though trapped in a cage, as though trying to get out. And how and why had he come to be on the beach? Hours had been cut out of his life and the missing hours worried him desperately. Had he behaved like a Hennessy or disgraced himself?

And now it was 6.26 a.m. and Carol was beside him, obviously scared stiff of him, looking at him in such a frightened way.

'Carol . . . What's happened?'

He didn't really want to know and somehow she was aware of that and didn't tell him.

'Carol . . . Is everyone all right?'

'Bruce is hurt, I think.'

'Badly?'

She shrugged. 'Could be. We don't know.'

'Colin and Mark?'

'They're all right, but what about you?'

He didn't answer. 'Have we got anything to eat?'

'No,' she said.

'To drink?'

'No.'

'We've saved nothing?'

'Nothing.'

He sighed, and that stranger inside him was still in a panic.

'Where are we, Gerald? Do you know?'

He shook his head.

'You *must* know.'

'Why must I? Why should I?' His voice was breathless and his manner was abrupt.

'Jan thinks we've gone south. She thinks that's why it's cold. Victoria, maybe, or Tasmania.'

'We're on the ground, aren't we?' he said, 'and we're alive. What more do you want?' He was trying very hard to behave well, but it was difficult.

'We've got to be somewhere, Gerald. Surely we can work it out?'

'Did you get the maps?'

'I told you we didn't get anything.'

'Can't do much without maps.'

'We were going to look for things, but – we were afraid we might find Jim.'

'Well, if you're afraid of that we'll never find anything, will we? Jim can't hurt you.'

'Don't be so callous, Gerald.' It was out so quickly and so thoughtlessly, and instantly she knew it was a mistake.

He looked at her coldly and his mood had completely changed again. She didn't know what he was going to do, didn't know what to expect of him, and suddenly she was very frightened. But oddly, he was the one who ran. The sand flew from his feet and he must have covered more than a hundred yards before he suddenly stopped and sat in a huddle, hopelessly confused, lost, lonely and tearful.

Carol hadn't even wished him a happy birthday.

11. Debris

'Jan!' It was Carol calling her, almost in an undertone. The call had special quality that Carol had never used before in the sounding of Jan's name. They weren't friendly enough for that. They didn't have much in common.

Bruce said, 'Go on; see what she wants,' and Jan went to her, but Carol moved several paces farther away from Bruce, drawing Jan after her. 'What is it, Carol?' she said.

'Gerald . . .'

Jan pulled a face.

'What do you think?' Carol asked her.

Jan didn't really think anything; all she had was a feeling and it was a feeling that she didn't want to share with Carol.

'Does he frighten you?' Carol said, as though it hurt her to say it.

Jan didn't care to explain that she'd never liked Gerald very much, anyhow. She couldn't talk about Gerald to Carol. Gerald Hennessy was a little tin god as far as Carol was concerned.

'And Bruce is hurt, too,' said Carol, struggling against Jan's lack of interest. 'He is, isn't he?'

'Could be. But he won't let anyone near enough to find out.'

'That leaves Colin and Mark. You can wipe Mark off, so it leaves Colin. And Colin's not much use.'

If that was what Carol thought, Jan felt duty-bound to take the opposite view. 'He did all right last night.'

Carol was becoming annoyed. 'I'm trying to say there are only two of us –'

'Three. You can't forget Colin.'

'All right! Three. Though I'd like to know where the third is. I haven't seen him all morning.'

Jan shrugged. Colin's absence troubled her, too, but she wasn't going to admit it to Carol. Then she said, 'What's the point of all this?'

Carol sighed. 'It seems to me, though it mightn't seem so to anybody else, that we've got to do something.'

'Like what?'

'Like . . . oh, I don't know. Like looking for salvage and food and water. Even if we do find Jim . . . We can't sit round here doing nothing.'

Jan continued to feel unco-operative, not that she had any cause to. What Carol had to say was not in the least unreasonable. It was more or less what she thought herself.

'And we've got to find out where we are, as well,' said Carol, 'Gerald doesn't know.'

'Well, that's it then, isn't it? If he doesn't know we've no hope of finding out.'

'Look, what have I done to upset you?'

'Nothing.'

'Well, why can't we pull together?'

That was the moment that Bruce started yelling, 'Hey, you two. Come here!' If he hadn't been feeling sore he would never have addressed Carol so roughly (Jan didn't count), and afterwards, when he thought back, he felt surprise that Carol hadn't objected. Instead, she came at once, trailing Jan after her.

'Gerald's really round the bend, is he?' Bruce asked.

'Of course he isn't,' snapped Carol.

'Well, what's he sitting down there for, like a booby in a corner?'

'He's miserable, that's all, like all of us. Like you, too. You've been doing a bit of a moan yourself.'

'Bruce is hurt!' Jan bristled. 'If you had an ankle like his, you'd be moaning, too.'

'What's wrong with his ankle? Is it broken or isn't it? Is he going to let us do something for him or isn't he?'

'I'm not having you mugs fiddling with it.'

Carol turned a hostile eye on him. 'You're supposed to be a Boy Scout!'

'What's that got to do with it?'

'Everything! You're supposed to help others. You're not supposed to be a nuisance. And you know Jan's a Guide.'

'So?'

'She must know something about it because she brought Gerald round last night. If it hadn't been for Jan, Gerald would be dead.' Jan didn't know what to make of that! Carol on her side. Then Carol said, 'Do you know anything about breaks, Jan?'

'A bit. I've got my First Class.'

'She's not a mug then, is she?'

Carol sounded much too masterful for Bruce; not at all like the girl in the aeroplane yesterday. He murmured almost sheepishly, 'O.K. then. Have a look at it.'

But Jan didn't really want to look at it. Not now that she had to – under Carol's eye – now that Bruce was prepared to submit himself. It was one thing practising First Aid on people who were not hurt; quite another trying to do it on people who were in pain. But there was no pulling back, just as there had been no pulling back last night when it had been Gerald.

She knelt and laid her fingers gently on Bruce's ankle, and felt him flinch. Suddenly, not knowing why, she snapped at him: 'Don't be a sook. I couldn't possibly have hurt you.'

She hadn't either, but Bruce sighed and shivered and made a great show of bracing himself. 'Get on with it, sis. Kill me if you like. What do I care?'

There was an awful temptation for Jan to squeeze his ankle hard, to make him yell, to make him leap, but she resisted it with a shudder, and carefully compared his injured ankle with his sound one and then with her own. 'I'm blowed if I know, but it seems all right to me. I know it's a nasty bruise and swollen and all that, but honest, Bruce, it's not broken.'

'I know it's broken.'

'You've made your mind up about it, haven't you?'

'Yes,' he said.

'And you're not going to be talked out of it!'

He was getting angry again, and so was Jan, and they glared at each other until they remembered, with some embarrassment, that Carol was still there and that Mark, too, was standing not far away like some unhappy looking object carved out of wood. 'And what do you want?' Bruce growled.

Mark looked at his feet. 'About Col's pants,' he said.

'His *what*?'

'Col hasn't got any pants.'

'For cryin' out loud,' shrieked Bruce, '*why* hasn't he got any pants?'

Carol said, 'Oh, dear . . .'

And Jan said, 'He took them off last night, didn't he? Crumbs, Col hasn't got any pants.' And she giggled.

'Is *that* where he is?' said Bruce, glancing at the fore-shore.

'Yeh.'

'Just because he hasn't got any pants?'

'Yeh.'

Bruce hooted. It was the first time he had laughed since yesterday.

'Colin said you'd laugh.'

'Did he?'

'Yeh . . . But it's all right for you. What's Col going to do? Where's he going to get some more?'

'He can't have mine,' said Bruce, 'if that's what you mean. Why don't you give him yours?'

Mark looked awkward and glanced at Carol and inspected his feet again. 'Don't be silly . . .'

'What's silly about it?'

'They wouldn't fit . . . He wants to know what he's going to do.'

'Go without, I suppose. There's nothing else that he *can* do.'

'He said perhaps Jan or Carol would make a lap-lap for him.'

'A what?' said Jan.

'You know, a sort of skirt, with slits up the sides. He said maybe you could make it out of a –' Mark swallowed '– a petticoat or something.'

'He said *what*?' bellowed Bruce.

'He's got to wear somethin', hasn't he? He can't go walking round in his underpants, not with girls an' all.'

'Why not?'

'He can't, Bruce,' said Jan. 'You know he can't.'

'I've never heard such rubbish in all my life. You tell him he can't have my sister's petticoat or my pants either. You tell him to go jump in the creek.'

'Look, Bruce,' said Jan, 'that's not helping Col, is it?'

'It's nothin' to do with us. It's Col's funeral. He shouldn't have taken his pants off in the first place.'

'But he did take them off and you know why.'

Bruce's mouth opened, then shut firmly. Then he scratched at his neck. 'Aw, crikey,' he said.

'Wouldn't it be best,' said Carol, alarmed by her own audacity, if we took a run along the beach to see if his pants have been washed up?'

Jan felt her heart flutter. Oh, what did Carol say that for? Why bring up that again so soon? Fears that girls shared were not meant for the ears of boys.

Carol said: 'Let's face it, Jan. Let's get it over. It'll have to be us.'

Jan felt sick, but Carol was so right. It was far better to face up to the issue of Jim and get it over and done with. And he mightn't be there, anyway, and then they'd be able to comb the beach properly for articles of value, quite apart from the matter of pants for Colin.

'Face what?' said Bruce. 'Get what over?'

'All right,' said Jan, 'I suppose so. You take that end and I'll take this.'

Carol had been going to suggest that they should go together, but that was the end of that idea. She wouldn't argue the point and make her fears so obvious.

'What the heck are you girls talking about?' Bruce said.

'Oh, nothing . . .' Jan took a couple of steps, then looked back to Mark. 'Coming?'

'Yeh.'

'Come with me, if you like,' said Carol.

Mark blinked with more than faint surprise and Bruce said quietly. 'Oh . . . Jim!' But not quietly enough. Jan glared at him and Mark's eyes slowly widened.

'Jim?' he said. He swallowed, and felt guilty, and looked to Jan. That was where his loyalties lay. 'I'll come with you.' And moved quickly, just in case that other one, that Carol, started being awkward. The only trouble was, Jan was heading in the right direction!

Carol watched them go, miserably, and glanced at Bruce. 'Sorry,' he said, 'you know I'd come if I could.'

Carol plodded off on her own along the curve of the beach that swept into the south. That was where Gerald was, still sitting on the sand. She went close to him but he didn't turn his head. He allowed her to pass and then watched her from the corner of his eye, his lovely Carol all bedraggled in a shrunken dress, moving from one piece of debris to another with an obvious and strange reluctance, then growing more distant, until suddenly he saw her run and drop to her knees.

Gerald sat up straight, intrigued, for the moment forgetful of himself, then almost at once slumped back into disinterest and despondency. He had no idea what was wrong with himself except that feeling miserable was easy and feeling any other way about anything at all was too much effort.

Jan, a couple of hundred yards in the opposite direction, picked up a soggy wad of paper. 'Colin's book!' she said.

'What book?'

'You know, *Oliver Twist.*'

'Show me.'

'Take your hands off it! You'll ruin it.'

'Funny girl, eh?' said Mark.

'No, I'm not being funny. If we're careful we'll be able to dry it out.'

'What for?' squealed Mark.

'Probably fall to bits, but it's worth the try It'll be a job for Bruce.'

'Whaffor, for Pete's sake?'

'Don't be *dull*. To read, of course. We might be here for ages.'

Marked laughed nervously. 'Don't be silly.'

'Ages and ages, maybe. There's no saying. It'll be good

having something to read.'

Mark's mobile face twisted into an extraordinary expression. 'Ages and ages? What are you talkin' about?'

'Just what I'm saying, that's what!'

Jan hurried on and Mark trailed after her reluctantly, whining: 'Ages and ages? They'll come for us, won't they? They'll come lookin' for us. They'll find us.'

He wanted to delay her, desperately wanted to hold her back. She was getting so awfully close to Mr Jim.

'No,' said Jan, not unkindly, 'you must know very well that they wouldn't know where to start. We're right out in the middle of nowhere, on an island or something. Way down south or way up north; Gerald doesn't know where we are. No one knows. And the sooner you get used to the idea, Mark, the better it'll be. We've got to start pulling together. We've got to work out some way of staying alive . . .' He voice faded.

She fell back and ran a few steps away, and Mark was left standing, pivoting on his heel.

Jan stammered, 'Not that way, Mark . . . Oh, Mark . . . It's poor Mr Jim.'

Mark felt a right proper rattlesnake, but didn't guess for a moment the real significance of what he had done. There probably wouldn't have been any squabbles at all if he had told them in the first place.

Carol came back and stood behind Gerald and Bruce yelled from the distance. 'What's that you've got there?' But Carol wasn't interested in explaining the obvious to Bruce. If explanations were needed for Gerald it would be different. In fact, she longed for him to ask her or to turn his head, to take some notice of her, and that he failed to do so hurt her rather than annoyed her. Surely this sullen, brooding boy, could not be the same Gerald who had

called for her yesterday at her home and had fought so
bravely to control the *Egret*? Or was he? For there was
that other Gerald who had turned from Colin in disgust
and who had been so slow to move when Jim had died.
Looking back, even farther, perhaps there had been other
times – when he had been dropped from the football team,
when he had flunked British History through absolute
carelessness, and after he had fallen, exhausted, during a
cross-country run. Not quite the same, but not completely
unlike it.

'My suitcase has been washed up,' she said.

'Has it?' But he didn't look at her.

'There's something in it for you.' She dropped a packet
on the sand beside him then bent and lightly kissed his
hair. She had never done anything like that before, had
never dared, but she meant it to say something that she
couldn't put into words. It meant, 'Gerald I'm your
friend; even when the weather isn't fair.' Then she drew
back from him hurriedly because she knew Bruce would
be watching and might laugh, and even Gerald might be
outraged, might flare and shout at her. There was something else she had wanted to show him, but kissing him
had sort of upset it, so she trudged up the sand to where
she thought Colin was hiding. 'Col,' she called.

'Yeh.'

She couldn't see him but the voice was there and surprisingly close.

'Would you wear a pair of my hipsters?'

'Jeans, you mean?'

'Not exactly. They're pink. But they are pants, you
know.'

'Gee,' came a wail from the bush. 'Bloomers.'

'No, no! Satiny things, but they've got long legs and a
zip up the back.'

There was a heavy pause and Carol glanced back at Gerald. She was sure he had the packet in his hands, simply from the attitude of his head. It had cost her three weeks' allowance. She hadn't even had a coke for three weeks. It was difficult getting something good enough for Gerald because he had so much already. Then Colin's head came round the side of a tree-trunk. 'Show me,' he said.

Carol held up the hipsters and Colin's lean face lengthened. It looked like a face out of a funny film. 'Gee,' he said.

'Do you want them or don't you?'

'They're *wet*.'

'Sorry; but you're lucky to get them at all.'

'Will they fit, do you think?'

'We're about the same size, aren't we?'

'S'pose so.'

'They'll be big for you rather than small. They'll be all right.' (Funny. She seemed able to speak to him without feeling awkward. He'd always seemed so stiff and starched. He wasn't really.)

'Pink . . . Gee whiz.'

'You were prepared to wear a petticoat, weren't you?'

Colin's face became redder and longer and he sighed, 'I'll wear 'em . . .'

Carol was by then aware of Jan in conversation with Bruce and of Mark a long way up the beach. Heaven alone knew what Mark was up to; why he hadn't come back with Jan. Carol tossed the hipsters at Colin's tree, then latched her suitcase. She wanted to go back to Gerald, but knew she couldn't. There was a limit to that sort of thing.

'Thanks for the pants,' Colin said.

'That's all right.'

'I'm awfully sorry I swore at you last night.'

'You didn't mean it.'

'I didn't either. I'll be careful with your pants, Carol. They're new, aren't they?'

'They were. They've been in the sea now and you might be wearing them for years, anyway.'

He came out from behind the tree but didn't notice the object in her hand. 'They're not too bad,' he said, 'I s'pose.' And stood and looked at himself. 'Well, I suppose they'll do if Bruce dosen't make it too hot for a fellow.'

'Blow Bruce,' said Carol.

'Yeh. Blow him. I knew he'd laugh about the lap-lap; but fellows look good in them. Polynesians and Indians and fellows like that.' Then he squirmed. 'Gee, they're wet ... What did you mean – I might be wearing them for years?'

She shrugged. 'Depends on where we are, doesn't it?'

He pulled a face. 'Well, that's something we've got to work out. Don't worry. We'll work it out. Don't you worry about that.'

His face was not as mobile as Mark's but expressive nevertheless, in a level-headed way. She began to dislike herself for belitting this boy. Perhaps he was going to be their real strength. After all, he had proved himself already, hadn't he? He might look a perfect sight but there was something of merit about Colin that even bony ribs and pink satin pants did not destroy.

'You've got blood on you!'

'Yeh,' he said, 'but it's nothing. When I saw it I thought my innards were fallin' out, but I don't even remember it happening. It's all right.'

It was amazing what a pair of pants, even pink pants, did for a fellow's morale. He took her suitcase from her and was surprised by its weight. 'What have you got in it – bricks?'

'It's all wet, Colin. And worthless, really.'

'Nothing to eat in it?'

'No.'

Then he saw the wireless set in her hand. 'Your transistor!' he screeched.

'That's right,' she said, with a widening smile that she couldn't hold back. She was an absolute stunner when she smiled like that.

'Oh, bless you, Carol,' he cried and dropped the suitcase and impulsively hugged her. Then suddenly realized that he had his arms around her and fell back embarrassed. 'Does it work?' he said, almost shyly.

'Not yet. I suppose it's too wet. We'll have to dry it out.' She offered it to him.

'It's a beauty,' he said.

'I know.'

'Short-wave, too.'

'It's a good set, Colin. It's Japanese. It wasn't very expensive, but it's a good one.'

'That means we'll be able to pick up Radio Australia and hear about ourselves on the news. If it's short-wave we've just got to pick up something, Carol, haven't we? Where do you switch it on?'

She showed him and he held it to his ear and turned the tuning knob. 'It sure doesn't work yet,' he said, a little more soberly, 'but I suppose it will when it's dry. Do you think it will, Carol?'

'Why shouldn't it?'

'It's been in the water, that's all. I mean, it mightn't be just a matter of drying out. Perhaps parts of it have been spoilt. Gee, wouldn't that be a blighter . . . Does anyone know anything about wireless?'

'Gerald you mean, or Bruce?'

'Gerald mainly. Bruce wouldn't. Bruce wouldn't know

any more about it than I do. Gee, I hope we can get it to work.'

He looked at her seriously, with a straight face and steady eyes and handed the set back to her. 'If there's a local station or anything coming in strongly we'll know where we are then. But it'll be awful if it doesn't work, Carol. Wouldn't it be awful, though.' He sounded rather breathless and they started back down the beach.

Carol had an eye on Gerald. She was edging his way rather than directly back to Bruce and Jan. Gerald hadn't opened his present; it was still on the sand beside him. Colin sensed her drift that way and said, 'What's biting Gerald?' Then he saw that she was close to tears. 'Aw,' he said, 'don't carry on, Carol. He'll be all right. He's been through an awful lot.'

'So's every one else.' She hadn't meant to say that, except to herself.

'Not the same way.'

'It is the same way. You were just as brave as he was.' She was vaguely surprised to realize that she meant it.

But Colin shook his head. It was all a bit hazy, anyway, and there were things about it that he didn't want to drag up into the light of day; the memory of them was disturbing enough. Then he was looking into Bruce's eyes – Bruce staring back, looking him up and down, though not with the good-natured insolence that was more typical of him.

'Carol's fixed me up,' said Colin awkwardly, referring to his pink pants. 'Not bad, eh? And she's found her transistor, too!'

'It doesn't work yet,' Carol said, 'but I'm sure it will when we dry it out.'

But Colin had become aware of Jan. Obviously, she had been crying. 'What's wrong?' he said.

She sighed. 'Col ... it looks as though you'll have to bury Mr Jim.'

In that moment Carol's heart went out to Colin, for he visibly stiffened and put her suitcase down with a jerky movement, as though his limbs were mechanical things.

'I see,' he said. That was something he had heard his father say in unpleasant situations. Then he added, not really meaning it, but hoping frantically for a response: 'Why shouldn't we do it together?' But he answered his own question breathlessly when no one else answered it for him. 'Yeh. It's not for girls, is it? Or for you, Bruce.'

Bruce flexed his leg and looked wretched.

'And certainly not for him.' Colin meant the Gerald he had hated when he had lain sick on the floor of the *Egret*. 'He's a dead loss.' Carol's sharp intake of breath hastened him on. 'Oh, not in everything. Not in everything. Just in some things. Where's Mr Jim?'

Jan pointed. 'That way.'

'What's *Mark* doing up there?'

'Digging in the sand.'

With what?'

'His hands.'

'What happened to the shovel out of the crash kit?'

'We lost it.'

'Well, someone had better look for it. It'll be out there somewhere. A shovel can't float away.'

'Look,' said Bruce, 'if the sea tore the *Egret* to bits it'd push a shovel for miles.'

'I don't reckon it would. I reckon a shovel's different. It'd dig in.'

Carol said, 'I'll look,' and went at once, running out to the wreck of the *Egret*.

Colin was trembling, but trying not to show it. 'You

know,' he said, 'we just can't dig a hole in – in the sand. It's got to be in – the ground.'

Bruce looked away. 'That's what I think. That's what I keep telling Jan.'

'And you can't bury people without a preacher. People aren't like scraps or dogs. They're *people*.'

'We've got to bury him,' Jan said. 'Things might get at him; it'd be awful. And we can make a cross. We can tie the pieces together with wire from the *Egret* ... We can't leave him there!'

'Who's been to a funeral?' Colin said.

Colin hadn't. Bruce hadn't. Jan hadn't.

'You're pretty good on the prayer book, Jan ...'

'I couldn't ...' Almost a panic hit her.

'Do you know what it says?'

'Only bits ... I can't remember that sort of thing ... I couldn't – conduct a service.' She sounded fervent, almost frantic.

'When I get him in the ground,' Colin said, 'we must assemble to say a prayer. It's got to be done right.'

'Look,' said Jan desperately, 'Bruce reckons there might be a town back there ... Do you think I should go and see?'

'There's no town,' said Colin. 'You know that.'

'But there might be,' Bruce said. 'If you don't go and look you'll never know. Crikey; we might be only a couple of miles from help. There'll be a parson there – and a doctor – and water – and food. After all, Jim's past danger. We're the ones that are in trouble now.'

'Look,' Colin said, surprising himself by his own vehemence, 'if there was a town there'd be houses on the foreshore and boats and litter and ... There'd be kids down here by now; it's Saturday. And don't tell me they wouldn't have heard us last night. They'd have heard the engine;

they'd have heard us crash. There's not even a homestead; there's nothin'; because they would have heard us, too . . .' By then he was breathless and his voice had gone up the scale to a thin pitch and he had caught sight of his pink pants and felt foolish and miserable and ill-used. 'Oh, crikey,' he wailed, and ran away up the beach towards Mark.

Mark was sitting on the edge of the hole. 'Swipe me,' he said. 'You look pretty.'

'Aw, shut up.'

'Anyway, pirates used to wear pants like that.' Then the subject lapsed, because Mark decided that Colin was not amused and when Colin was not amused he sometimes got rough.

'Where's Mr Jim?'

'Over there. Behind that dirty big rock . . . It's going to take all day to dig this hole, you know. Six feet under. That's what they say, isn't it?'

'Something like that. But it won't do here.'

'What won't?'

'The hole.'

Mark was immediately indignant. 'Course it will. It's a bloomin' good 'ole.'

'You're hardly above the high tide mark, you drip.'

'I *am* above it!'

'The beach won't do. It's got to be way back. Way back from the sea.'

'Yeh? And who gets him there? Who carries him?'

Colin hadn't though of that, and regarded his kid brother with faint respect. Mark had used his head, or Jan had, or someone had.

'And how are you going to dig back there, anyway?' Mark went on. 'It'll be hard up there and there'll be tree roots and all to cut. I know. I'm good at diggin' 'oles.'

'Yeh,' said Colin. Mark was, too. His backside had been tanned a dozen times for digging holes under the house and behind the fence, and once, with a pick, clean through the kitchen drain.

'And apart from anythin' else,' said Mark, 'I've got a bellyache. I'm hungry.' He didn't feel squeamish any more about Mr Jim, now that everything was in the open. 'I'm awful hungry, Col. Aren't you?'

Colin nodded.

'So we dig the hole here, eh?'

'No we don't.'

'Fair go, Col. All me work an' everything?'

'It's got to be done right. Proper ground and prayers and a cross and – and respect. You'd want it done right for you, wouldn't you?'

'I'm not dead. I'm not goin' to die ...' Then Mark slumped, outwardly and inwardly. A great, shapeless black shadow seemed to wrap itself around him like a blanket. After a while, with drooping mouth, he looked up at his brother. 'Gee, Col ... I s'pose we'd better try. See if we can find a place that's not too hard, eh? I don't fancy much diggin' with sticks.'

12. Somewhere

The spade had dug in just as Colin had said it would. That was how Carol found it, dug in deeply at an angle, with the top of its handle barely above the sand, and after she had wrenched it free, by sheer good fortune she found the tomahawk as well, a few inches away, in the spill of oil from the *Egret*'s engine. Then she called Jan.

'There's no saying what's buried round here,' she said. 'I reckon this is the spot where we should look. I reckon we should dig the sand over foot by foot before the tide comes in.'

'But Col wants the spade.'

'I know, I know. But what's more important?'

Jan wasn't sure.

'Look, even Bruce reckons we should worry about ourselves, and the way the tide's coming in, it'll be up this far in half an hour. I know what Col would say. At least, I think I do. And I think Jim would say the same, too; Jim, of all people. I'd say we've only got an hour to save everything along the beach or it'll be gone. I reckon everybody should get on to it; Col, too. Don't you, Jan, honestly?'

'What's the use? It's all a lot of junk. It's all smashed up.'

Carol drew a deep breath. 'We can put it together and make a hut out of it, can't we? And there's no saying what use we'll find for other things ... We might find more

146

clothes – and we're going to need them, I think. There's not much in my case, only girls' stuff. And we might find things that we can cook in.'

'Cook what?'

'Please Jan. Don't let's fight about it. We're wasting *time*.'

They were, too, but there was a stubborn streak in Jan that didn't want to go Carol's way in anything, or anybody else's way either. It was such an effort to *talk*, to *do* anything, to walk, to think, even to argue; but argue she did. 'I think it would be more to the point if you got Gerald on his feet; great big loafer he is. Is he scared to soil his hands or what?'

'You leave Gerald out of it.'

'Why should I?'

'He's sick.'

'Sick, my fat aunt. If he's sick I'm sick.'

Carol glared at her. 'You're sick, all right. Real *sick*. Do you want to die or something? Don't you want to help yourself? You're a real prawn, Jan Martin.'

Jan could see herself all the time and hated everything that she saw. But she sneered, 'Yeh?'

'Ych!'

'Hey,' bellowed Bruce from the beach, 'you two at it again? Turn it up!'

Carol, on impulse, suddenly flung the spade at Jan's feet, so close to her feet that Jan had to jump to save herself from injury. 'Go on,' Carol shrilled, 'take the spade to Colin. Take it yourself. What do I care if you want to cut your own throat?' And she started walking as the words started coming, away from Jan, away from Bruce and Gerald, away from them all; she was fed up with the lot of them.

They were nothing but petulant children. She felt so

much older than the oldest of them, though but for Mark only months were between them. To bother any more with them was beyond her will or her patience. What on earth was wrong with them? What on earth was the matter with them?

She walked south, alone and determined to be alone, far along the beach, deliberately ignoring the scattered wreckage, not even stopping to recover a sand-encrusted garment of uncertain description that caught her eye, unaware over a considerable distance of the tomahawk still in her grasp; in fact, until then, probably unaware of anything but a torrid condemnation of her friends that broke over her silence, that had her mumbling and murmuring to herself. She was tempted to throw the tomahawk furiously away, but a saner instinct withheld her, and for a minute or two she stopped, hands on hips, conscious of the uncomfortable build-up of sand in her shoes, of the fast-stepping gulls that had preceded her, and of the surprising proximity of the headland that from the area of the *Egret*, had seemed so far away.

She glanced back and couldn't see the others at all, then at last counted them off, three of them, at a much greater distance than she had at first supposed: three figures, three specks, almost indistinguishable from rocks.

Carol pulled off her shoes, emptied out the sand, tucked them under her arm and walked on in her stockinged feet, until the stockings, too, began to annoy her. They were in an awful state – she simply hadn't noticed them before – and all at once all her clothes seemed to be shrinking, seemed to be constricting her and irritating her. They were all crumpled and creased and sticky. She felt a longing to be wholly free, to be out of sight of the others completely, perhaps to get beyond the headland and there to bathe herself clean in the sea.

A new light, diffused sunlight, lay on the sea, and the colours out there were swiftly changing from leaden hues to living greens and blues. Cloud was melting away; perhaps in its greater depth it had passed on and the scum that was left was dissolving into the heat of the day; for there was heat in the air now; real heat generating with the showing of the sun.

She thought of thirst and hunger, of breakfast in the nook at home. She supposed it was about eight o'clock, Saturday breakfast time. Perhaps there wouldn't be any breakfast at home this morning. She thought of her mother and father and her stride lost its purpose. Oh dear; what a state they'd be in. How would her mother behave? She'd be hysterical, probably; inconsolable probably. A woman without backbone, that was her mother; a small, fluffy, silly, slightly brassy sort of woman running to fat, whose world was fashion magazines and hair-styles and diet plans and a blind conviction that she was beautiful. But she had a heart for all that; there were many mothers less motherly. Poor woman; she'd be desperate. All her eggs were in one basket. Carol was her first-born and last-born, her only one. She'd be sobbing; inconsolable. (A new word for Carol, but there it was again.) Her Dad would have his hands full; he'd have no time for thoughts of his own.

Carol's stride was slow, pensive.

It was very hot; all of a sudden, very hot. Stifling. She had a feeling that perhaps she should not stay in the sun; that it would be dangerous to become thirsty to a greater degree than she already was. She had thought a little along that line before but now took it further. There was no water, no milk, no cokes, no tea, no coffee, no hot chocolate. None of the fluids that before had ever been more distant than the kitchen or the refrigerator or the garden tap was to be had for the taking any longer.

Carol stopped and spoke aloud. 'It can't be true. How can it be true?'

It was so difficult to grasp. Maybe that was the trouble with everybody. They couldn't *grasp* it. They could talk about it, but not *really* understand it.

Had she read somewhere that it was safe to drink a little sea-water in emergencies like this? Or was it the other way round – that sea-water was always dangerous, never to be touched? Oh, the things that one forgot; the things that one should *know*. How to light a fire, for instance, without matches. Which shellfish to eat and which to avoid. Which wild berries were food and which were killers. How to trap birds. How to hunt animals. How to catch fish without a hook and line or net.

The explorers of years past had gathered dew from the grass in the early morning; they had eaten grass and rats; the roots of grass and the seeds of grass.

'My great-grandmother was an Aboriginal. She knew where to look for food; she knew where to find it. Perhaps it's still in me. Perhaps it's something that will wake up. Wouldn't it be strange if it did?'

She looked at the backs of her hands, at her fingernails, at her arms and feet and toes. She had a white girl's body, a white girl's skin, a white girl's mind and a white girl's instinct. Nothing of the Aboriginal was left; it had been bred out; it had been lost in white generations. What a shame.

A heritage such as that could have saved them. Then what could her mother have said about that? Then what? Then she might have forgiven her husband for the alien blood in his veins.

Should she give it a try? Should she walk into the bush and try to remember, try to stir up the past? Should she perhaps lie with her heart to the hungry ground and wait

for the awakening of the instinct that would lead her to
the roots and seeds and pith of plants that had nourished
those distant generations of primitive men, to the honey
ants and wild bees and tiny animals and fat white wood
grubs and to sources of water underground?

Perhaps it was worth a try. If she didn't try she'd never
know. But if the instinct did awake, how would she explain it to Gerald, to Jan, to Colin? Particularly to Gerald.
His feelings about that sort of thing were so fiercely
formed, yet so contradictory. His feelings argued with one
another. They were the feelings not so much of a boy but
of a man set in his ways; his father's feelings, probably.
The Hennessys, she suspected, thought not so much as
individuals as a clan.

Perhaps she should not try it.

Hesitantly, she walked on towards the headland. Rocks
lay out there where the land met the sea and great breakers
were crashing over them, and beside her was the land itself,
shrouded by woody, twisted trees. She didn't even know
what sort of trees they were. And grass too; clumps of stiff
grass. (Species unknown.) And dryness, brittleness; not
exactly desolation, but there was a feeling of immense
and deep distance, of singing silences over a vast and un-
inhabited land. Flat land it seemed to be, a coastal plain
too harsh for men.

She climbed into the headland rocks, electing to stay
back from the sea. There was danger out there in the
eddies, the spray and foam and exploding surf. She came
on to a grassy prominence almost as hard on her feet as
the rocks, and moved across its brow until the coast continuing beyond came into her view.

It was as vast and as featureless and depressing as the
land behind her. At least it was at first, for at first she
could not see it all; but suddenly she saw a line of boulders

stretched into the sea; a line so straight and purposeful that only the hand of man could have put it there. It was a breakwater, a harbour for ships!

Carol was spellbound. A pain hit her in the middle like the blow of a fist. Her mind, in frantic disorder, suddenly drove her back across the headland to wave for the others, to shout into the wind, to scatter the gulls over her head. She shrieked into the north but nothing was there to hear her. The beach was empty, quite empty, for as far as the eye could reach.

She ran back to the other side, excited and confused and laughing, and scrambled down through the rocks and slipping sand, twice dropping her stockings and shoes, then running when she reached the flat until there was a stitch in her side that caught her breathlessly somewhere between agony and joy. She had to stop, her body twisted to one side, panting, her impatience with herself a peculiar sort of pleasure. 'Oh, Carol,' she groaned, 'a stitch at a time like this.' And she hobbled on towards the break-water, towards the unmistakable channel that betrayed a tidal stream, perhaps even a creek from the inland flowing down to the sea.

A fresh water creek? A river? A wide stream up which launches and small ships moved back and forth? Where people on this hot Saturday morning would be drifting idly in little boats, trailing lines in the water, fishing the sandy bottom? A port for livestock? For export beef? Or bringing in supplies for a scientific expedition? Men looking for oil perhaps, or prospecting for minerals? Was Bruce right all the time; was there a town back in there, upstream? But no single possibility did she pursue. The only thing she cared about was the fact that they were no longer lost. Not lost at all. People were here. There'd be help to bury Jim, a proper place to bury him; medical attention for Bruce. Food and water for all of them. A telegraph station or a wireless to send news to their parents. Excitement fragmented her thoughts; had them rushing in all directions; clouded her mind. It was her imagination that saw for her. Her eyes saw only in part.

She came breathlessly to the edge of the tidal stream, thirty feet or forty feet wide, and already the salt swell was running inland back into an area of surprisingly dense growth, into a tangle of boughs and roots and foliage in places low enough to meet the water. At first sight it was a jungle, a shock, a steaming wilderness, a swamp, screeching with bird life, humming with insects, crawling with reptiles, as though flashed suddenly and thunderously on a screen in a dark theatre. But the sound was an illusion; the sound wasn't there, except in her own head.

Carol was bewildered and her panting gained the immediate depth of a moan of despair. But it *was* a breakwater; it *was* a port. Her eyes traced the boulders out to sea, thousands of boulders built into a wall. But there were breaches in it where storms had smashed through; breaches that no one had repaired. And there were no buoys for ships to moor, no little boats at anchor, and the jetty was derelict. The jetty she had seen was in truth a few piles long abandoned, encrusted with shells, draped with weed, standing like broken columns, like broken monuments eroded by time, mysteriously growing shorter then longer as the swell heaved past. There was something about it now that expressed a finality, an isolation and a hopelessness that she had not known earlier. This was a dead place; a place where men had failed or perished; not a place to which men sailed but from which men had sailed away.

She felt desolate, marooned, cast away. It was a load

upon her, a great weight upon her. 'Daddy . . .' she choked, and stifled the word.

But upstream something was taking her eye, almost speaking to her, repeatedly, as though trying to attract and hold her attention, until finally she saw what it was: an arrangement of overgrown rocks, perhaps a wall.

Almost at once she felt faintly uneasy, as though the wall were a living thing or a personality that she should at all costs avoid. But it drew her, first commanding her curiosity, then her steps. Flowers were growing there; the first flowers she had consciously seen. Leaves were there, different kinds, the kinds that one might expect to see where plants had been placed by men. But all was over-grown, feverishly overgrown, straggly, wild, neglected in a way that the untouched native bush never appeared to be. This was a dead place, dead for perhaps a century; remembered only by ghosts.

It was a wall all right – there were four walls, partly fallen down, formed of beach stones plastered together with crumbling lime mortar, enclosing a tangle of rotten wood and long grass; fallen timbers, once rafters perhaps, once a roof over unknown men. Traders? Settlers? Stock-men?

On the stone lintel, over the doorway, was carved a date: *1874.*

Carol stared at it, half guiltily, as though she had been ordered not to.

1874.

Oh, a long, long time ago. Long before her own time, long before her parents' time, way back in the unreal days when her great-grandmother had been young; days that had happened outside of Carol, beyond her. *Before Carol.* Another world entirely; but spinning through time on this beach.

Frightened people, were they? Or fearless and tough, dressed in coarse flannels as thick as boards, with wide hats, and scarlet kerchiefs knotted at their necks. Rugged voices. The laughter of men; echoes of that odd and raucous laughter that she could never accustom herself to. Or was there then the same sagging stillness as now; the same beat, like a dying heart-beat, of the ocean on the shore?

Carol bowed her head and squeezed shut her stinging eyes.

13. Birthday Present

The three children didn't cry any more. Even the tears on the inside – that didn't show on the outside – had dried up. In a way they had grown harder; in another way weaker. Colin, in particular, was drawn and unnaturally pale. It had been something of a humiliation to discover that Jan was physically more able than he was; her body was deeper and broader. Her body didn't creak and groan, didn't seem to seize up, didn't seem to suffer pain from digging or from dragging heavy weights.

'Mark,' Colin panted, 'maybe you'd better go to Gerald.'

'That's not a job for a little kid. That's not fair.'

'Please, Mark.'

Mark knew what it was all about. He'd seen Colin like this before; grey, wrung out. Colin worried the family on occasions.

'Go on, Mark,' Jan said. 'I reckon it should be you, too.' She thought, mistakenly, that she knew what was on Colin's mind. Col was pretty deep at times; cunning in a way. He could see *ahead*.

'Aw, swipe me,' Mark said, but he went.

On the way he stopped to talk to Bruce. (Mark could be cunning, too.) Perhaps he could use Bruce to solve his problem. 'How's the book going?' he said.

'Drying out all right, I think, though all the glue's come unstuck. We won't be able to read it when the wind's blowing!'

'What about the wireless? Col says.'

'Dry. But I'm blowed if it works.'

Mark scratched his itchy head with a distinctly nervous mannerism. 'Comin' to the service?'

Bruce seemed to stiffen, seemed to hunt around for something to say. 'It's hot. I'm melting. They could pour me into a can. Guaranteed Pure Bruce Dripping. You tell 'em to come and shift me before I get sunstroke or something.'

'Comin' to the service?' Mark repeated doggedly.

For a moment Bruce seemed angry, then looked away to where he had smoothed a yard or two of sand and drawn a map of Australia with a twig. He had marked in the borders of the States, the great inland lakes and all the coastal features that he could remember. He didn't answer Mark's question. 'It'll be a start,' he said instead, 'to work out where we are, though I reckon we're in the tropics somewhere; yeh. But everything's back to front. The sea shouldn't be in the west; and where are all the palm trees and everything. I mean, after all, we couldn't have flown right across the country to Western Australia. Unless that's why the wireless doesn't work. Perhaps we're too far away to hear anything at all. Or we could be here –' he put a finger on the Gulf of Carpentaria. 'But I don't see how we could have got that far, either. But we are in the tropics, you know; that's why it got dark so quickly last night.'

'Be a sport,' said Mark. 'Answer me.'

'How *can* I go to the service?'

'Perhaps Gerald will give us a hand and you can hop between us? Then you'll get out of the sun.'

Bruce stretched a leg. It wasn't all that painful, not really; it was better than it had been an hour or two ago. He'd been thinking of crawling into the shade, anyway, and would have done except for a streak of cussedness. First of all he wanted Jan to be absolutely sure that he was suffering. He had a feeling that she still didn't believe him. Maybe if he did hop all the way, grunting and groaning, Jan would be conscience-stricken. 'O.K.,' he said, 'you get Gerald to help and I'll come.'

Mark went on and sat a few feet from Gerald, just above the line reached by the incoming waves. After a while, Mark said, 'Hi.'

'Hi,' said Gerald, and he didn't sound too bad; almost friendly. 'Bruce wants to go to the service,' Mark said, 'and I need your help to get him there.'

Gerald didn't look at him, but turned his face enough for Mark to catch his profile. He looked all right from the side; much the same as always. 'Service? What's that?'

'We're going to have one. Jan's going to say some prayers. She's pretty good at that sort of thing.'

Gerald turned his head away again and seemed to sag from the shoulders, as in fact he did. Far away, on the curve of the beach, he could see a tiny figure that must have been Carol coming back. 'For Jim, I suppose?'

'Like Col says, we'd want it done right if it was for us.'

'I don't know that I see the point.'

'Well, we've dug a grave an' all. It was awful hard, Gerald. Not the ground, I mean. You know, diggin' a grave.'

'Yeh; but what's the use?'

Mark choked. 'He's in it! It's his *grave*.'

Gerald had had an idea that they had found him. He was not surprised, though he made out to be. He looked Mark in the eye. 'You should've told me. Someone should've told me you'd found him.' And that was true enough. He'd wanted them to ask him for help, but they hadn't done so. He'd wanted someone apart from Carol to show an interest in him. He didn't like being on his own, being out of things, but he had wanted the move to come from them. After all, it was his birthday and he'd saved all their lives. They'd all be dead like Jim but for him.

Mark said, 'It was awful getting him there, Gerald. Jan did it, and Colin and me.'

So they'd sent Mark to him; hadn't come themselves. Maybe they'd sent Mark to shame him.

He couldn't look Mark in the eye any more.

'You'll help me won't you, please Gerald, to get Bruce there?'

He swayed on to his feet and it wasn't put on. He was weak and sore and terribly miserable and burning with shame. 'Yes,' he said, 'I'll help.'

'What's that on the ground?' said Mark. 'You've dropped something.'

'No I haven't. Carol dropped it.'

It was the packet.

'Well, we'd better not leave it there.' Mark picked it up. 'It's wrapped in birthday paper,' he said. 'It is yours, isn't it?'

Gerald shrugged.

'And you haven't even opened it . . . I had a present for you, too, but I lost it. It was a beaut tie, a real humdinger. Go on, open it, Gerald. See what she's given you.'

That was something else Gerald had wanted to do, to open the parcel, but something had stopped him.

Mark thrust it into his hands. 'Go *on*. See what it is.'

Gerald felt awkward about it, but opened it just the same. The gift-paper wrapping had been quite wet when Carol had put it down beside him, but now it was brittle dry and tore with a crackling sound.

'Is it spoilt?' said Mark.

'Don't know what it is yet.'

It was a small jewel case of white plastic, not much larger than a matchbox, and in it was a silver tie-pin in the shape of pilot's wings.

'Gee, whiz,' said Mark, 'that's beaut.'

'It is, isn't it,' said Gerald, 'it's nice,' and felt bad about it. He had seen it in the shop window. He knew how much it had cost.

'She likes you, doesn't she?' said Mark.

Gerald's lips became tight and he slipped the little case in his pocket.

'It would have looked good with my tie. It was a real humdinger, Gerald. Mum picked it out. We had to take the first one back to the shop 'cos I picked that. Mum said trust that old skinflint to foist the rubbish on to a kid. Mum said it'd never do for the likes of Gerald Hennessy.' Mark rambled on because he didn't know how to stop. 'Mum says you can pick what a fella's like by the tie he wears; even if someone else has bought it for him, Mum says. Do you reckon that, Gerald?'

'Yes,' said Gerald. 'That's right.'

'Why, Gerald?'

But Gerald was looking back to where Carol was coming along the beach. He hadn't heard; hadn't heard a thing; and Mark felt foolish and uncomfortable and went on his own to Bruce.

'How'd you get Gerald to come?' Bruce said.

'Asked him.'

'*That* all?'

'Carol's given him a beaut tie-pin.'

'Crumbs,' said Bruce, 'I'd forgotten his present. Had a set of Indonesian stamps for him. Real beauties they were. Birds. On a first day cover and all. Never find 'em now, not with the tide back in and all.'

Gerald arrived, obviously at a loss about practically everything. He couldn't meet Bruce in the eye. He'd never been embarrassed in Bruce's company before, because Bruce wasn't that sort of fellow. You usually felt naturally free and easy when Bruce was around.

'Happy birthday,' Bruce said.

Gerald's smile was a thin one. 'Thanks.'

'I've lost your present.'

'That's all right. It's not your fault.'

'First day cover it was. A beauty. I'll see if I can get you another when we get back home. Maybe the stamp shop will have another.'

'Thanks,' said Gerald. 'Whose wireless is that?'

'Carol's.'

'Does it work?'

'Dead as a bloomin' doornail.'

'Sea-water, I suppose,' Gerald said, 'in the batteries.'

'I've dried 'em out. Everything's dry. Perhaps we're just too far from a station.'

'It'll be the batteries.'

'Do you know or are you just guessing?'

Gerald shrugged. 'Guessing, I suppose, but I reckon I'm guessing right. How about you? Can you walk on that ankle?'

'I reckon I can hop.'

'It's a long way,' Mark said.

Gerald looked back down the beach again. 'Carol will catch up, I guess,' he said. 'I don't suppose we need to wait.'

They helped Bruce on to his feet and bore all the weight for him that they could, though the fact that Mark was so much shorter made it awkward. It need not have done, but then it was too soon for Bruce to admit – even with surprise – that his ankle might have got him there without assistance.

Jan came back to where Colin was sitting in the shade, patiently fashioning the cross. 'They're coming,' she said, 'all of them!'

Colin grumbled, 'I wish they'd done it a couple of hours ago . . . Gerald, too?'

'Yeh.'

'Must have got over his sulks.'

'Or you shamed him into it?'

They regarded each other with frankness and something like respect. 'Jan . . . You're all right.' He said it in a way that pleased her, that for the first time in her life seemed to lift her up beside Carol. She had always been in Carol's shadow. 'Can you remember those prayers?' Colin said.

Jan sighed and at once felt less sure of herself; fluttery, frightened. Colin could be so stubborn. He'd asked her the same question several times and she had given the very same answer. 'Have I got to?'

'I reckon. Yeh, I reckon.' And he went back to the cross again, binding its two members with wire from the *Egret*. It was stiff and springy, not easy to handle; Jan had had a real battle hacking it off with the spade.

'I don't know what religion he is, do I?' Jan said.

'Does it matter?'

'Of course it matters.'

'I don't think so.'

'He might be Catholic or Protestant or anything.' Jan was trembling.

'Don't see that it matters.'

'Well, it does.'

Colin shrugged. 'We'll have to get a nice tidy bit of metal from the fuselage, too, and scratch an inscription on it. Bruce does pretty good printing, doesn't he?'

'When he feels like it.'

'Well, it's something that he could do. If he can't get round on his feet it's something that he could do for us, isn't it?'

'I suppose so.'

Jan was a rare one all right; a hard person to talk to. When she was busy with her hands she was quite different. Look how she'd jumped in that hole and dug like a navvy.

Carol at last caught up with the others while they were resting. Gerald and Mark were the ones who needed the rest, not so much Bruce; in fact Bruce was wondering – simply from an awakening sense of what was fair and what was not – whether he should start hobbling along on his own. He felt that he might manage with less effort, anyway, than hopping on one foot.

'Thanks for the lovely tie-pin,' Gerald said to Carol.

Her tired face immediately brightened. 'That's all right,' she said.

'It's nice. Really nice, Carol.'

She smiled again.

'But you shouldn't have spent all that money.'

'I wanted to.'

She hadn't meant to embarrass him, but she did, and he could find nothing more to say.

'Where have you been?' Bruce asked.

'Round the headland.'

Bruce sensed, somehow, from her tone of voice that something was wrong beyond that headland. 'We're all going to the service,' he said, with an inflection in his voice that said to Carol, almost as if she had heard the words: 'Tell us about the headland later.'

'The service for Jim?' she said.

'Yeh.'

'So nothing's been saved? Nothing's been picked up?'

'Odds and ends, but first things had to come first.'

'I reckon the other things should have come first.'

'I wouldn't have thought so. Not from the way you stalked off.'

Carol bit her lip. How like Jan Bruce could be. 'I had my reasons,' she said, 'and your sister knows them better than anyone.'

'Lucky you didn't do her an injury when you chucked that spade at her. Blooming silly thing to do.'

'I didn't *chuck* it.'

Bruce said, 'We can't make your wireless work.'

Carol slumped a little and Mark said, 'Come on; we'd better get along.'

'I'm going to try to walk,' Bruce announced.

'What?' squealed Mark.

'Got to pull my weight, haven't I?' said Bruce stoically. 'Got to try sometime. Might as well be now.'

They helped him up – that much he felt he should permit – then pushed them away. It wasn't difficult, though he took care to make it look heroic. There was pain, of course, but pain in reverse, spasms of it not coming in but going out like the jerks of a twisted rubber band. After he had gone through the act he caught the look on Carol's face. If anyone had been impressed, it wasn't her. In that instant, Bruce vowed he'd limp for the rest of his life if he had to, to convince her of her error.

Colin and Jan stood side by side at the head of the grave and the others stood at the foot, Bruce vaguely cross because Jan hadn't taken any notice of him. They bowed their heads, not then because of reverence but because they were shy of looking at each other, shy of reddening eyes and of their uncertainty. They didn't really know what they were doing.

Colin said thinly, 'This is going to be a proper funeral; as proper as we can make it . . . Do you know what religion he was, Gerald?'

Gerald drew a sharp breath and after a while said, 'I don't know – I don't know that he was any.'

'I'm sure it makes a difference . . .' It was Jan, with her voice breathless and breaking away.

Then all was quiet and hollow and strange, except for gulls and waves beating and heat. The heat was there like another person, like another presence. They sweated from the heat; Carol for a heady moment felt faint from it.

Colin's hand at last crept out and held Jan by the wrist. 'Go on,' he whispered.

But she couldn't. She tried to start, she tried and tried, but there wasn't a thought in her head; just a frantic emptiness. And Bruce knew; he looked up at her and saw her and prickled with discomfort.

Colin waited and waited in growing dismay, his heartbeat almost stifling him, a sharp-tasting remembrance of his sickness in the *Egret* welling up. Someone whimpered; Mark, he thought; and Jan was panting, drawing great breaths and trembling so violently that it frightened him. He squeezed her wrist desperately, trying to urge her, trying to force her, but not a word came out of her.

His own jaws were trembling, his tongue was dry, but he drove them to speak for him. The voice didn't sound like his own at all. 'We're here to bury Mr Jim Butler. He was a nice man. He liked to fly in the sky . . . I suppose he did like it, did he, Gerald?'

'Yeh. I suppose so.'

'God made the sky and everything else that Mr Jim liked, too, I guess. He – made Mr Jim as well so must have known about him. Trouble is, I don't know whether Mr Jim knew about God – an' all . . . Did he?'

'Golly . . . I don't know . . . Well, he must have done, mustn't he?'

'Mr Jim didn't have time to – say good-bye to his friends or anything. He died all of a sudden like . . . But I reckon God must have been there because if He hadn't been we would have died, too. I mean, Gerald's never flown an aeroplane properly before, on his own, has he? I reckon God must have been there all right, so if He was there afterwards He must have been there before . . . Aw gee . . . Jan; say the prayers . . . say something.'

Jan shook. She had never prayed out loud, except as one of a crowd or to read from the printed page. She had known it would happen. No voice. Nothing there. She was so ashamed.

Mark started crying because he didn't like the silence or Colin making a fool of himself, and every one else standing round shifting their feet and breathing heavily and not knowing what to do. Then Carol said hesitantly: 'Forgive us for not being able to pray properly to you for poor old Jim. But we've never been to a funeral before. We don't know what to say.'

Then she wondered whether it was right and decent to go on, whether she might make of Jan a more bitter enemy than she already seemed to be, but even while she wondered about it her words stumbled on.

'He was so manly and so clean. He had such a nice look about him. He couldn't have had a face like that if he was a bad man; he couldn't have had a light like that in his eyes if he'd been ugly inside.

'And thanks for bringing us here, the rest of us, in safety, but forgive us for being nasty to each other. And for forgetting that Gerald was marvellous and that Bruce kept us calm and that Colin got us ashore and that Mark has been so very good. And for forgetting that but for Colin and Jan, Gerald would be dead like Jim. We'd be putting him in the ground, too.

'Thanks for bringing us here to try to do the right thing for Jim, because if we hadn't come together like this something awful might have happened to us. I don't know what; but something was beginning to happen; something was going wrong. Even if we starve; even if no one ever comes for us . . .'

All at once that seemed to be the end somehow, or the beginning of the unknown, and the words dried up, stopped. In a while Jan started stammering the Lord's Prayer, and Gerald, as though groping in a fog, pinned his silver wings to the tie wires of the cross.

14. Too Far and Too Many Sharks

Gerald's watch, a good automatic, had alone survived the rigours of water and sand, and by the time they started back to where they had slept the night it was just on ten minutes past eleven.

They started out together, but little by little fell apart, straggled along in pairs, each keenly aware of every other person, but shy. In a way they felt they knew each other differently from ever before; in another way they were silenced by the shyness that had begun in Carol's words and had worked outwards from her into them all; a shyness that drew them together in obligation to each other, but tangled them up when they tried to talk. It wasn't a cold feeling, it was a warm one, but *awkward*. Jan felt it was like looking into a mirror and finding that the reflection there was not only of herself but of everybody else as well. (A distinct improvement.)

They came back to where they had started from, Jan and Bruce last of all; Bruce limping, and not needing to act the part, either. He stretched out on the sand thankfully, but the others stood round as though waiting for something to happen.

Gerald started out to speak in a formal way, twice started, but stopped. He had been going to say that he was sorry, but then felt it didn't really matter; everyone knew he was sorry; they didn't need to be told. Carol had cleared the air. To apologize would be to look back; stir up things that were better left where they were in the past.

Then Mark flopped down and drew circles with his fore-finger, not exactly sad circles, but pensive ones. Carol fiddled with her wireless for a while. What a singularly useless thing a wireless was when it wouldn't make a noise. It was an awful shame. It really was. Then she opened her suitcase and spilled out its contents, and self-consciously – because every one was watching her – separated them to dry in the sun. Colin looked them over; all girl's things, but there was a blouse that might do him at a pinch. Then he caught sight of Bruce's map in the sand. It was too small, he decided, too crowded, so he smoothed a larger area and began to draw another one, eight or nine feet across. Jan was hungry; her stomach rumbled and ached and she wanted to talk about it, even complain about it, and there was Mark, only a yard or two away, putting stems on his circles, making them into apples. Jan felt so hot, so hungry, and she was beginning to feel *dry* in a most disturbing way.

'I reckon we ought to have a swim,' she said, and looked round, almost surprised that the voice breaking the silence was her own. 'Don't you? It'd cool us off.'

'Yeh,' said Colin, 'perhaps we should.'

'Well, I reckon we ought to sit in the shade, anyway,' Bruce said, 'it's stupid sittin' here. We don't have to live here just because we slept here, do we?'

That was a point. It was like walking into the wrong house at night by mistake, then waking up in the morning and calling it home.

'We'll all get sunstroke or dehydrate or something if we stop here,' Jan said.

'What's that?' said Mark.

'What's what?'

'Dehydrate?'

Jan sighed. 'I don't know, exactly.'

'We've got to have a plan,' Gerald said, 'I think that's agreed, isn't it?' (It was good to be able to join in again, even though it was an effort to sound natural.)

Colin looked at him, relieved, as they all were, that Gerald was trying to be himself. 'Yeh, we've got to do some planning, Gerald, like working out where we are. Take this map –'

'You'll never do it, Col. There's more to it than you think, you know.'

'Well, we can try. Then we've got to decide whether we stay here or start walking.'

'Mustn't leave here,' said Gerald. 'Never leave the scene of the crash. That's a rule, you know.'

'Why?'

'Because it's wreckage that they come looking for, and wreckage is easier to see than people. Not that there's much left of the *Egret*, is there?'

'We could collect it,' Bruce said, 'what's left of it, and make it look better, couldn't we? Make it into an S.O.S. perhaps.'

They thought about it and Colin said, 'It's an idea, all right. Make an S.O.S. out of stones, anyway, a good long one, say a hundred yards long.'

'Crumbs . . .'

'Well, it wouldn't take long, not if we all helped.'

'All depends, though, doesn't it,' said Gerald, 'on where we are? They mightn't come looking here, might they?' (It was a foolish thing to have said. He wished he could call it back.)

Colin prodded his map. 'We're up here somewhere, I reckon, in the tropics.'

'So do I,' said Bruce, 'and we're looking out west into the Gulf of Carpentaria, from a coast that runs north and south.'

Colin was surprised; that was something he hadn't expected from Bruce. 'Cape York Peninsula,' Colin said, 'that's what I reckon, too. We're down on it somewhere. A thousand miles from Coonabibba. We are, you know.'

'We *can't* be. I didn't fly that way. I headed more west than north.' Gerald was beginning to feel that he belonged again. 'Look, I know something about these things, not much, but enough to know that you can't work it out without proper maps. You've got to know the exact distances and wind speeds and courses and all sorts of things. Honest, Col, I wouldn't lie to you. You've got to have instruments; parallel rules and protractors and dividers and mathematical tables. Gee, navigating an aeroplane's a pretty big thing.'

'It might be, but we are facing west from a north-south coast, like Bruce says. That's common sense. You don't need anything fancy to prove it.'

'There are hundreds of places you can face west from – bays and inlets and estuaries . . . Look, if you say the Gulf of Carpentaria, I could say New Guinea or up in Indonesia somewhere.'

'Now you're making it silly. We all know the *Egret* couldn't fly that far.'

'Why couldn't it? It couldn't fly to the Gulf of Carpentaria, either, without a dirty great tail wind behind it. And we had it, I'm telling you. We had a beauty.' He shouldn't be saying these things and he knew it He had a responsibility and he wasn't honouring it, but the thought seemed to demand that it should be stated. 'We could be almost anywhere at all. I don't know which way the wind was blowing and we've no hope of finding out now – nor then, either. Unless that wireless will work, and I'll lay any odds you like that it won't. It wasn't a party, you know. I didn't know what way I was going. I didn't think we'd even get out of it alive . . .'

Then he caught sight of Carol, frowning, warning him not to start looking back. Perhaps to make sure that he didn't, she said, 'There's an old settlement past the headland, but no one lives there any more.'

'A *what*?' said Colin.

'A breakwater and – and stone houses all fallen down.'

'You're kidding.'

'I wouldn't kid about that.'

They stared at her then all started talking at once and Bruce managed to get the last word. 'I told you there'd be a town, didn't I?'

'It's not a town. Nothing like it. It's dead.'

'You mean a ghost town?'

'No, I don't mean even that.'

'Just round that headland!' said Jan. 'Just down there?'

'Why didn't you tell us?'

'Crikey. Let's get crackin'. What are we stopping here for?'

'Yeh, let's get moving. Let's get everything together and get moving. How far you say? Just round that headland?' Colin started bundling Carol's clothes back into her suitcase. 'Come on, everybody; grab your shoes and all.'

'Please,' cried Carol, 'it's a dead place. No one's been there for ages and ages. We've got to be sensible. We've got to be careful, even.'

'Careful?' echoed Bruce.

'Snakes and spiders and scorpions and all that sort of thing.'

'Aw, come off it, Carol.'

'Well, you've got to think of these things. That's where you find them, in – in broken-down old places. It's creepy. I was frightened.'

'Oh, Carol!'

'Well, I was, and you will be, too. I think we ought to stay away from the place, that's what I think.'

'You can't expect us to do that,' Gerald said. 'What'd you tell us for, then, if that's the way you felt about it?'

'Yeh, that's silly, Carol,' said Colin. 'I mean, if there's a town there must be water, mustn't there?'

'It's *not* a town. It never was. 1874; that's the date I found. Nearly a hundred years ago.'

'But there must be water!'

'There's a creek, but it's salt.'

'And probably things we can eat, growing there,' Jan said. 'Bananas, maybe. Coconuts. Things like that.'

'Flowers, that's all. Only flowers. Everything grown over and spidery. Flowers all run wild; thousands and thousands of marigolds and sunflowers. And they're all along the beach, spread everywhere. I didn't see them going. I saw them coming back. *Flowers*, but nothing you can eat.'

'You can eat sunflower seeds.'

'Can you?'

'Of course you can,' Jan exclaimed. 'You know that, Carol. They make cooking oil out of them and all sorts of things. And like Col says, there must be water there somewhere. There must be a well or a spring or something. Once we start looking we're just bound to find it, and maybe a house, too, good enough to live in – after we fix it up a bit.'

'Live in?' wailed Mark. 'Swipe me, we're not going to stop here for ever, are we?'

Suddenly, everything seemed to be different. They were excited and Carol got caught up in it despite herself. Their renewal of good spirits was so infectious that even

her annoyance with herself for failing to recognize sunflowers as food didn't last overlong. She was annoyed with
herself for being so helpless where practical matters were
concerned. She could put words together, but not actions.

She was annoyed with herself because Jan had thought of
the seeds and she hadn't. Carol had the blood in her veins
but Jan had the instinct! Of course, sunflowers were not
native to the country; white men had brought them in;
but that was a poor sort of excuse. Fancy imagining that
lying on the ground might awaken an instinct in her,
when Jan didn't even have to stop to think. Jan just knew
it or did it without hesitation. She did things like bringing Gerald back to life, and knew things about sunflower

seeds – and that people and fresh water went together. But walking along with them all, cheerfully, took the sting out of it.

Gerald walked with Carol and carried her suitcase; it was not that they were separate from the others, but Gerald managed to keep close to her, sometimes brushing her with his free hand. The physical contact added to his confidence in himself, for his mind was not without its worries, not without its after-tastes of failure; his leadership had never been tested before and he hadn't come out of it well. Colin had come out of it better, but it was Carol who was strong in the things that mattered, even though she was a girl. That was what Gerald decided. Physical strength didn't matter, not with a girl. Carol seemed to have strength left over for others to draw on. He had never looked to her as a source of strength before. He had looked upon her as someone to impress with his cleverness. She was an unusually pretty and personable girl, and if a fellow was to be seen with a girl at all, better with her than another, because she was a cut above the rest in town.

So he walked beside her and brushed her with his hand and smiled when she looked at him and tried to give the impression that he was still the Gerald of old. But with the others it was different. (Carol forgave completely, but they didn't.) Something had risen up again, though maybe *they* didn't know it was there. It wasn't like a wall or a fence or a high mountain, but something was there that seemed to make them more distant. For they walked as in a crowd with laughter and chatter (and occasional flashbacks into sadness) and impatience – impatience because Bruce was so slow; but sometimes when Gerald spoke no one listened. It wasn't that they snubbed him; they didn't hear. It was like being a little boy again trying to get a word edgeways into a grown-up conversation.

'You know, looking at this thing the way we should,' he said, 'I don't know that we should have left the crash so soon.'

It got through to Carol but Jan cut in with something about food. Eating sunflowers, she said, would be like chewing up a mouthful of teeth, if they couldn't boil them first to make them soft. 'And who's got some red-hot spit to start the fire?' Her coarseness jarred on Gerald.

Colin said, 'I reckon we ought to go fishing. We could make spears and try throwing them from the breakwater.'

'Or bird-nesting,' shrilled Mark.

'Off the breakwater? What sort of nests would they be?'

'Well, if we really are up north,' Bruce said, 'we might find turtle eggs, mightn't we? You know, you dig 'em out of the sand. And what about turtle soup? They say that's beaut.'

'And oysters,' said Mark, 'maybe with pearls in them. Would a fella die if he swallowed a pearl?'

'Or crabs.'

'Crab meat's poisonous.'

'Don't be silly.'

'It is, you know. Isn't it Jan? You've got to be careful with crabs.'

Later, Gerald said, 'Goanna meat's not bad if you cook it right. I've tasted it.' But then the conversation had turned to other things.

Bruce said, 'We didn't make that S.O.S. or collect up the wreckage either.'

'Plenty of time,' said Colin. 'If we're as far from Coonabibba as we reckon, they won't be searching up here for days.'

'I wouldn't say that. They're bound to spread the search out, pretty soon, you know.'

'As far as this? Rats. Don't forget that they'll be thinking that Mr Jim was flying it. They'll never dream that we're up this far because old Gerald did the flying.'

In a while, Gerald said, 'Parts of the wreckage might be useful for cooking pots and things.' But then Jan started up on history.

'1874 you said, Carol, didn't you? If we put on our thinking caps we might crack it. If it really is a deserted coast – except for this settlement . . . Well, there can't be too many like it, can there?'

'It might be a mining town,' Bruce said, 'and there were hundreds of those, you know. They sprang up and died down. Hundreds of them.'

'On the *beach*?'

'Well, why not?' Maybe it was a port for a mining town farther upstream. You said there was a creek, didn't you, Carol? I still reckon we might find a town back inland a bit.'

'Particularly if there's no fresh water, you mean?'

'Yeh, that's right, Carol; you took the words out of my mouth.' (She hadn't, but it wasn't the sort of thing a boy could admit to a girl who hadn't known you could eat sunflowers.) 'Yeh, if there's no fresh water there must be a town farther up.'

'There might be crocodiles up the creek,' said Mark.

'If there are, boy, you'd better watch out, or we'll throw you to them.'

'Do crocodiles lay eggs?' Mark wondered. 'I reckon it would be beaut to eat crocodile eggs.'

'Crocodile eggs! Yeh, they lay 'em; same as kangaroos.'

'Aw . . .'

'They *do* lay them, Bruce,' Jan said.

'Kangaroos do?'

'Crocodiles!'

'Come off it, sis. You're as soft in the head as he is . . .

What are we going to do about cooking pots? Has anybody given *that* a thought?'

'We haven't got anythin' to cook yet, have we?'

'Maybe not, but you've got to prepare. You've got to think about these things. You can't hold a handful of water over the fire to boil it, can you?'

They were not paying attention to Gerald and he wasn't used to it. They would never know, ever, what he had been through. He was quite sure of that. For six hours he had carried the weight of the world on his shoulders. Then he had broken. If they remembered anything, they remembered mainly that he had broken. The rest was a bad dream largely beyond their recall.

In the old days he had been the centre, like the sun with planets in orbit, simply because he was Gerald Hennessy. Then for six hours, like a giant, he had burst the bonds of boyhood and become a man. But the strain of remaining like a man had been too great and because of it he had become a planet himself, and a not very important one at that, so far out from the centre that sometimes they forgot he was there. But when Colin spoke they listened; when Jan spoke they listened; when Bruce spoke they listened; even Mark got a good-natured hearing. There was a moral in it somewhere. Gerald couldn't put a finger on it, but something older and wiser was taking root in him.

Then, out of nowhere, he remembered setting 000 degrees on the compass of the aircraft. Remembered so distinctly setting it and for hours flying it. He undoubtedly had gone north – not west at all – just as Bruce and Colin had said he had. How far north? A great distance; that was plain to see. New Guinea perhaps? He had not been serious when he had suggested it.

New Guinea might be dangerous. In remote and inaccessible parts it was still a savage land. The last savage land on earth, he had heard someone say. There were people who ate human flesh; people who fired poisoned arrows. People in warpaint and plumes and with bones through their noses. There were deadly snakes and malaria mosquitoes and swamp fevers. Perhaps this settlement past the headland had not been abandoned but wiped out?

Gerald said, 'I reckon we should do something about arming ourselves. I mean it, you know. With clubs and spears and stones for throwing and things like that. To be on the safe side.'

'Whatever for?' Carol exclaimed.

'Just to be sure, that's all. It could be New Guinea, you know. I did fly north. I've remembered.'

By then it was well past noon and the sun rode high and the headland was close and their shadows on the sand were very short.

Bruce got left behind after they crossed the headland and saw the breakwater. He wanted to run, too, but it wasn't in him.

'Wait for me,' he shrieked.

But they didn't.

'You lousy lot,' he yelled. 'Wait on . . .' But they streaked away from him, Colin and Jan out in front (Jan ran like a boy), then Mark, then Gerald with Carol's suitcase banging against his leg, then Carol. Carol wasn't made for running in fleet-footed company. That was obvious. Bruce had noticed before that some girls, even slight and shapely girls, lost their grace when they tried to run.

'Hey, Carol,' he bellowed, 'What's the hurry? You can wait, surely?'

Then was appalled by his own cheek. She was Carol Bancroft, after all, even if she did run like a duck. But she waited, apparently not reluctantly, and Bruce hobbled up to her floundering for the right words to say. 'Strike me pink,' he panted, 'you'd think they were running for a prize. And there's nothing there, is there? You said there was nothing.'

'Not much,' she agreed, 'nothing to get excited about, anyway . . . It's just that it looks good from here. I thought it looked good from here, too, first time.'

He had called her back and now he was alone with her. And almost tongue-tied. What a fellow could say in a crowd and what he could say after the crowd had gone away were two different things. She was such a smashing girl, even all wind-blown and bedraggled and hot like this. Poor old Jan looked like a red-faced yokel beside her. 'I – I didn't think it'd be so far,' he stammered. 'I'm about done in. This leg, you know.'

She took his arm and helped him along. (Golly, he hadn't meant that.) From the weight that bore on her she knew he wasn't shamming. 'Do you think that Gerald could be right,' she said, 'that we're in New Guinea?'

It was pretty good, that pressure of her hand on his arm. Carol Bancroft holding Bruce Martin's arm!

'Blowed if I know,' he said. But he was letting himself down badly. She had asked his opinion. It was up to him to have one. 'It's a horrible thought,' he said importantly. 'And what can we do about it? I mean, we just can't walk out of here. If we don't know where we are, we don't know which way to go, do we? But I can't see how Gerald works it out. Honest I can't. I didn't think tail winds could do that.'

'Are you worried about it?' There was a degree of concern in her voice, as though his opinion counted.

'I suppose I am. Well, aren't you? I mean, we could be here for years. Really and truly years. We could grow up

here, even, just the six of us. If we don't get sick first, or
killed, or anything.' He looked at her tenderly, then said
hesitantly – willing himself not to say it but saying it just
the same, 'We might end up marrying one another some
day. Well, some of us. There are only two girls and one's
my sister and I guess you'd want to marry Gerald, anyway.'

His earnestness embarrassed her. 'That's silly talk,
Bruce,' she said. 'It could never come to that.'

'It isn't silly talk. Not if you think about it. You hear
of that sort of thing and it can still happen, can't it?'

'People getting married?'

'Being left here to grow up! Not finishing school or
having bands to listen to or books –'

'We've got *Oliver Twist*.'

He pouted. 'And a wireless that won't go! Bloomin'
thing! But having to make our clothes out of bark and
needles out of fish bones and . . . I mean, there are spots
like this where people just never come. Thousands of
square miles and people just never come here for jolly
good reasons.'

Her hand had dropped away from his arm and they
weren't walking any more. The shyness had gone. Something else was there. 'Carol,' he said, 'what if it's an island?
There are hundreds of islands up here, even big ones, and
no one lives on them and no one goes near them. I mean,
you know that. We've learnt about that. Places not fit to
live on. What about Molineaux Island. The settlement
they had there. No one knew it was there for ages and ages
until some pearlers put in for water and found all the
ruins and graves and bones and everything. Everybody
reckoned they were making it up until some history bloke
dug out the records. Everybody on Molineaux had died
of some sickness or other about a hundred years ago . . .'

He saw suddenly into her mind with that dismaying

intuition of his. 'Carol,' he said, and weakened. 'You don't think –?'

'Well, it could be, couldn't it?'

Jan felt frightened again, breathless, with an uneasiness that wouldn't settle on any one thing but darted about in all directions; an uneasiness that didn't want to ask questions but was surrounded by mysteries.

It wasn't a settlement at all. It was as though men had come here just for the sake of a stupid fight against the bush, just to show how clever they were, just to show how brave they were, but had never looked like winning; had been whipped and beaten and broken and stamped on. They should not have come here – any more than she should have come here.

They were not nice ruins, like the ruins she saw in photographs, all softened with ivy, not age-old ruins of nice places where people had been happy a long time ago. These were strangled ruins, where people had been lonely and desperate and cut off. Mad people, surely. If not mad before they came, mad before they got away; or dead before they got away.

Nothing was the way she had thought it would be; even the creek was just an arm of the sea or a tail of the sea, now seventy or eighty yards wide, surging inland, rushing and hissing among the trees. And what sort of trees were they that salt water didn't kill? Trees rooted in ooze and sand and salt; trees with unhealthy appetites, that's what they were. Somehow, she'd thought there'd be gentle sands, but the tide was in, high, and the sands were swallowed up, and it seemed as though the tide could come higher yet and press her back into the bush, perhaps pin her there, imprison her there.

It was the disappointment, the cruelty of it, the let-down.

Carol hadn't said it would be like this. Old, she'd said, and dead, but not strangled. And still being strangled years after it was dead. For a while, at the graveside, Carol had seemed to Jan like the best friend she'd ever had, because Carol had saved her from complete humiliation. Carol had cleared up so many things, put so many things right, but now she had come into the wrong sort of reckoning again. Carol had told them of this place and then had tried to talk them out of it. But she hadn't tried hard enough!

It was horrible, like the half-seen places that terrified Jan in her dreams. Even the idea of eating sunflowers now seemed like the absolute end. They were so garish, so unreal, so harsh. They didn't *want* to be eaten. All they wanted to do was glare.

'Let's go away,' she said, in a little voice.

'But fancy people living here?' Colin was looking round again, squinting and twisting his mouth. 'Whatever for? Whatever would they do here? How can you imagine it being a town or anything, ever? What'd they do with themselves?'

Mark came out of the scrub and said he'd found the ruins of four huts and a chook house, but if they thought he was going to live in any of them they had another think coming. 'It's sad,' he said, 'isn't it? Real sad. Even for the chooks it must have been.'

Gerald was nervous and couldn't stand still. 'We've got to be sensible, you know. It's all right in some ways.

'What ways?' said Jan sullenly.

'For the search planes. Better than where we were. It's the sort of place that'd draw the eye. The breakwater, and all, and a long line of rocks on the sands made up into an S.O.S.'

'I reckon Carol shouldn't have told us.'

'That's silly, Jan. We'd have found out, anyway.'

'But there's no water or bananas or coconuts or anything.' She didn't want to go into details, she feared details, but they started tumbling out just the same. 'You can't drink the creek water; it's salt. We've got to find fresh water and something to eat. Whatever are we going to do if we don't? You had something yesterday, Gerald, but Col and me, we were *sick* . . . And we've been working hard. And I'm thirsty. Not just ordinary thirsty. I don't like being thirsty the way I am.'

Colin said, 'Gee, Jan. We'll find something. I'll bet you we do, as soon as we start looking.'

'But we've been looking all the time. All the time we've been looking, all morning, everywhere. I mean, there hasn't been a minute that we haven't been looking; not really. We can't eat the leaves off the trees. We're not caterpillars.'

Mark laughed.

'Shut up,' said Jan.

'Whaffor? What have I done?'

Colin scowled. 'Yeh. Shut up. We've just got to start looking harder, that's all . . . I don't know; for a while I thought things were going to be all right.'

'We were fooling ourselves,' said Jan.

'But we haven't really tried,' said Gerald, 'not *really* tried, have we?'

'You mightn't have done,' Jan snapped, 'but we have; and we're sunk, that's what.'

'We'll sure be sunk if you keep on saying it.'

'It's the first time I've said it!' Jan was beginning to flare. 'It's the first time I've even thought it.'

'O.K., O.K.,' wailed Colin, 'simmer down, Jan. Keep your hair on, Jan.'

'I wish he'd killed us all in the aeroplane. It'd have been quicker. It'd have been easier.'

'Come off it, Jan. For cryin' out loud . . .' Colin's laugh was half-cry. 'Look, we're not dead yet.'

'Well, let's get away from this place. It gives me the horrors.'

'Where to?'

'I don't care where. Anywhere. Let's start walking round the beach. I don't care.'

'Gee,' said Mark, 'it's not all *that* bad, Jan.'

She started crying.

'We can't go, can we?' Colin said to Gerald, almost helplessly.

'Of course we can't. It always happens when people leave the crash. They get lost. It's the end of them. Golly, m'dad would kill me if he thought I was even thinking of it. We've got to stay here. We've just got to. We've gotta sit tight. Look, even if we sit here and wait for six months we've gotta wait.'

'I don't know,' said Colin, 'we seem to be thinking of things all the time but not doing anything much.'

'That's because there isn't anything much we can do. We can put out the S.O.S.; we can scrounge around for something to eat and drink; and that's it.'

'All right,' said Colin, 'let's do that much. Let's get on with it or we'll all go screamin' up the wall. I know just how Jan feels. I don't blame her one bit. It's this hanging around and doing nothing that's the trouble. We all get steamed up to start, then something happens, and we do nothing.'

Then Bruce and Carol walked into the picture. They'd been coming into it for a while, trudging nearer, and

Bruce called, 'I reckon I know where we are. We've worked it out and you're not going to like it.'

'Oh, golly,' groaned Colin.

'Molineaux Island. That's what we reckon.'

Bruce flopped down, panting, rubbing his leg, and caught sight of Jan, 'What's she blubbing for?'

'Where the dickens is Molineaux Island?' said Gerald, 'and how'd you work that out?'

But Colin stood quite still for a moment or two, looking out over the breakwater, then ran his eyes back along the sweep of the stream, past the old stone walls and the tangled bush, towards the shimmering unknown of the inland. '1874,' he said, then looked at Jan, because history had always been her strong point. Every one in her form at school knew Jan had a flair for history. And Jan had heard Bruce and was wiping her swollen eyes on the back of her hand. 'What do you think, Jan?' Colin said.

'Where is Molineaux Island?' Gerald asked impatiently.

Colin sounded irritable. 'In the Gulf of Carpentaria! Crikey, Gerald!'

Jan had got over her tears; she'd rubbed them away; sniffed them back; but still looked harassed. 'I hope not,' she said, 'crumbs, I hope not. That's the place where those pearlers put in for water and couldn't find a drop. All they found was a sea wall. A *sea wall*. Yeh; that was all they found, a sea wall – and bits . . .'

'How far to the mainland? Do you know that, Jan?'

She had become suddenly aware of a grave responsibility. They were going to accept as gospel what she said. To Gerald's question she replied, 'About fifty to sixty miles, I think.' Then she wondered and added: 'But *hundreds* of miles from anywhere settled. Too far to swim. Too far and too many sharks.'

'The Gulf of Carpentaria!' Gerald seemed to be

stunned. Even after he had remembered flying north his
thoughts had been tempered by doubts. No matter what
he had said, no matter what he had thought, there had
always been the feeling that it didn't have to be true and
probably wasn't. 'Are you sure, Jan? *Absolutely* sure, I
mean?'

This was a challenge and she had to face it with a level
head. And the fact that the challenge was there helped her
to compose herself. 'Well, let's look at it,' she said. '1874
was the date they founded the settlement all right. By
1878 they were dead. What of, no one knows. Sickness of
some sort. They were members of some religious sect or
other. The Saints of – of – oh, something or other they
called themselves.'

'But that doesn't really prove it, does it? That doesn't
make this place into Molineaux Island?'

'Well, there's the sea wall and the marshes and the
cottages – what's left of them – and the date and the creek
and the – the *sunflowers*!'

'Yeh,' said Gerald, almost blankly, 'sunflowers. Yeh, I
remember the sunflowers.'

'It fits,' Jan said. 'Everything fits.'

'So it's Molineaux Island?'

'It fits, doesn't it?'

'That's what I said in the first place,' grumbled Bruce.

'But how do we get off it?' Mark cried.

Colin felt all choked up. 'I don't suppose we ever do
unless someone comes and takes us off.' (Mark flinched
visibly.) 'Gee, this is sort of bad . . . It's one thing being
on the mainland and sitting tight, but being on an island;
on Molineaux . . .' Colin didn't know how to finish.

Not realizing it, they had started edging away, even
Bruce, back to the narrow strip of open beach.

'What did those people die of?' said Gerald. 'Could the germs still be here, do you think?'

'Golly, we've been climbing round all the old stones and everything –'

'It's an awful long time ago, though, isn't it?'

But they continued to edge away, quite openly now, not hiding it from each other.'

'Look, Gerald,' Colin said, 'you reckon we mustn't leave the crash, but are they going to look up here? I don't see how they'll ever think of it. They don't know anything about Mr Jim being dead. It'd be like losing something in one town and looking for it in another. It doesn't make sense.'

'But it's the Golden Rule!'

'It might be, but not up here. If we were anywhere on the mainland, yes, but not here. They think a pilot was flying the plane; not just any pilot either, but Mr Jim. Put out the S.O.S. and everything, sure; but leave a note to say which way we've gone. We've got to find somewhere better than this. I reckon we ought to get right away from here. What I'd really like to do is build a raft.'

'Well, you can forget that. That's plain silly.'

'What's silly about it?'

'That'd be the end of us, good and proper. To start with, we don't even know how to build one.'

'I know how to build one,' said Bruce, 'so does Jan.'

'Forget it,' Gerald said deliberately, 'we might as well jump in the sea and drown ourselves and be done with it.'

'Look,' Bruce went on, 'all we need is a few oil drums and some rope, and something for a sail. We've got a tomahawk to chop down trees, and a little bit of rope, and there must be vines and creepers about that'll do. And we can make a sail out of our clothes.'

'That's a real bright idea, that is!'

'Well, let's think about it, Gerald,' said Colin.

'What is there to think about? Oil drums, he says. Where do we get oil drums from?'

'There are the petrol tanks. We might find them, mightn't we? They might get washed up even yet. Things are washed up for weeks after a wreck. If Bruce reckons he can build a raft I reckon we ought to let him try.'

'Well, I won't be on it, I'm tellin' you.'

'Be blowed to you,' Bruce yelled, 'give us a chance. Don't knock it before we start it.'

'But it's so stupid,' Gerald cried. 'If what Jan says is right, what good is it going to do us? Even if you build one, even if it doesn't sink first time you push it into the water! There are six of us. It'd have to be as big as a house. And how do you steer a course? What if the wind blows the wrong way? What if we drift out to sea? What are we going to eat? Or drink? What if a storm blows up? And what about sharks? Strike me pink, Bruce, it's the craziest idea I ever heard of. I'm not knocking it for the sake of knocking it; honest I'm not. It's just plumb crazy. At least we've got dry land under our feet. At least we've got a chance; but out there we'd have no chance at all ...'

He had beaten them into silence. Their expressions were as harassed as Jan's had been.

'What we really ought to do,' Gerald added, calmly enough, 'is to start food gathering, lay out the S.O.S., set up a camp and get a fire going. And I mean not just talk about it, I mean do it.'

He felt no need of Carol's strength any more. He had enough of his own.

15. S.O.S.

Mark was becoming very sleepy, but he pushed off into the scrub along the foreshore to hunt for birds' nests. He would much rather have curled up in the shade and gone to sleep. It was funny being so tired at half-past two in the afternoon; as tired as he used to feel late at night. He thought of his room at home, of his bed, of his mum: 'You're to keep your hands clean and hair tidy and *not* to belch after meals.'

'Gee,' he murmured, but went looking for nests just the same, though he was a bit on the wary side, careful where he stepped, alert for snakes and creepy crawly things, often returning to the beach to make sure that someone, at least the sea wall, was still in view. He found nests here and there, but no eggs in them, no birds at home. Perhaps it was the wrong time of the year. And he didn't see too many birds, either, flying round. Maybe it was so hot they were all asleep.

He was *so* thirsty. It hurt him to swallow. He didn't want to swallow, but kept on doing it. He would try to think of other things, then suddenly find himself doing it again, swallowing. He chewed leaves for a while but they were bitter and didn't seem to help, though in fact they did.

It was a hard, stringy, dry bushland behind the foreshore where he was. Farther on it was more low-lying; the

salt-water marshes were down there and he was frightened
of them and didn't go that way. If there were birds' eggs
down there they would have to bally well stay there. He
wished he had gone fishing with Colin.

Colin had made spears, borrowing the tomahawk from
Jan to sharpen them. They looked all right until he tried
to throw them. He couldn't flight them well, but took a
handful off to the sea wall, nevertheless, and carefully
picked his way out over the rocks looking for fish. Tropical
waters teemed with fish; that's what everyone said; shark
and dugong and stingray and groper. Though they'd all
be a bit big for wooden spears. He was sure it would be a
hopeless sort of feeling to be hanging on to the end of a
spear stuck in a 600 pound groper! Or into a great big
turtle; except that the spear would bounce off, of course.
It was silly to be nervous of fish, but he half hoped he
wouldn't see any. They were bigger than he was. Big
enough to swallow him whole.

The tide was still well up and vigorous and Colin felt
too weak to be sure-footed. Perhaps later; perhaps when
he felt stronger he would dare to be brave. Then he would
stand, as he had seen pictures of aborigines standing,
poised on tip-toe at the water's edge, quivering spear held
high.

There were shellfish of different kinds anchored to the
rocks as if riveted to them, and he started belting at them
almost with shame, chipping them off, but he felt it was
all so futile somehow. What would they do with the
beastly things? Eat them raw?

Bruce, too sore and dispirited to join the scramble of a
food hunt, started gathering up rocks and arranging them
into the S.O.S. After a while he felt he had picked the
tougher job, not the easiest, but plodded grimly up and
down, back and forth, slowly forming huge letters about

thirty feet wide. Plodding back and forth almost in a trance.

Jan shifted everything of value back along the beach about 300 yards closer to the headland and tried the wireless again, longing for music or the voice of an announcer, but there was nothing. She was tempted to look for a sheltered camping spot under the trees, and in fact started clearing such a place with the spade until she grudgingly admitted that their survival probably did depend upon their ability to see or be seen, as Gerald said. Gerald had gone to great lengths to stress that point, even though Jan still felt faintly rebellious. Anyway, there were ants in the bush, and flies, millions of them, and the open beach was less plagued by the persistent little pests. So she picked a spot and felt moved to mark it out like a house, running grooves in the sand with the spade: a front door and a back door, a living-dining-room, a room for the girls and a room for the boys, and a kitchen. She thought that perhaps later on she could add a pantry (when they had something to put in it) and more bedrooms, an entrance hall, sunroom, and so on. She could turn it into a real mansion with private bathrooms and marble staircases and all sorts of things; a grand place like film people lived in. Then she got mad with herself for her childishness and became tearful, and turned her face away in case Bruce saw her, because he was trudging past, scowling, dragging his feet, hugging a stone to his chest like some primeval youth bent on murder.

In the kitchen she made a fireplace out of rocks, then went off to gather twigs for the fire and came back with such an armful that she used some of them to define her rooms more clearly. Then she thought of standing larger pieces up on end, pushing them deeply into the sand, to make walls for privacy. The rooms should be properly

separate, after all. Her mum would expect her to do everything right; not to be lax or anything. Then she got mad
with herself again, and tearful once more because there
seemed to be so many complications, so many that they
churned her up inside.

She squatted in front of the fireplace and stared at it,
at the dead grass and twigs so carefully set in best Girl
Guide fashion. There was one fly in the ointment; a Girl
Guide's skill was measured by her ability to light a fire
with a single match, not without matches at all. Some
native peoples rubbed sticks together, others twirled a
stick, others knocked stones together.

Jan continued to stare until everything became a blur.
By then, too, her lips were beginning to swell. Presently
Mark drifted in, empty-handed. Jan didn't know he was
there, and he didn't tell her. He felt guilty because he had
been sure he would bring back lots and lots of eggs. All
he had found was an old bottle, a very, very old bottle
that once might have had spirits in it or medicine. The
glass was green and thick and crazed. Perhaps they'd be
cross with him because there weren't any eggs. Col might
understand, Jan might understand, too, but it was Gerald
he was worried about. He couldn't work out what had
happened to Gerald. Gerald had become bossy all of a
sudden.

Then Jan saw him. 'Hi,' she said, as though her voice
came from a long way off.

'Hi,' said Mark.

'No eggs?'

'Couldn't find any.' He felt awkward. 'I found a bottle,
though. Do you think I should have another look?'

Jan turned back to her heap of grass and twigs and
wondered whether fire might come down from Heaven if
she prayed hard enough. 'No fire, either,' she sighed. And

she started rubbing sticks together, because with Mark there she felt she should try. 'A bottle,' she said. 'What sort of bottle?'

'A real old one, see. Old as the hills.'

It was not what Jan had suddenly hoped for. She had hoped for a nice bright bottle that might have worked like a magnifying glass with the sun shining through it. A good hot spot of light might start the fire.

'Are you making a house?' Mark said.

'Yes.'

'I like the rooms. It's a beaut idea. Will I get some more brush for the walls?'

'Would you?' said Jan.

'I'll say. I reckon it's a beaut idea.'

So she put the stick aside and said to herself, 'I've got to get the fire going. There must be another way.'

Gerald came across the headland dragging something behind him, then manhandled it over the rocks with a clatter on to the beach. Bruce, lying flat on his back, immediately sat up and saw him. 'What's he got?'he called. And Colin, way out on the sea wall, looking that way, wondered much the same thing.

Bruce limped off to meet him. It was part of the wing section of the *Egret*. 'Crumbs,' said Bruce, 'we can't eat *that*.'

Gerald looked worn out. 'I've been everywhere,' he said. 'It's a rare sort of island. We ought to be caterpillars, you know, like Jan says. There's nothing to eat but the leaves off the trees.'

'There are still the sunflowers.'

Gerald grimaced. 'It's just a dirty great desert. No animals or anything. I can't work it out.'

'What've you got the wing for?'

'To make dishes out of. Something to carry water in.

Get the metal off and it'll be dead easy to bend into any shape we want. But I can't work out why there's no water lying around.'

'Jan said that, didn't she?'

'The soil must be too sandy or something. It must go straight down. It should be lying around at this time of the year, up here. I mean, rain up here comes down in buckets.'

Bruce shrugged. 'Like we said, it's the real end of the earth.'

'Well, what did the aborigines do? How'd they live on it?'

'Who said they ever did? Maybe it's just one of those places. Real bad land. It happens, you know.'

'But the trees and grass and all?'

'Trees'll grow anywhere, give 'em time. Grass too. Crikey, trees grow out in Central Australia, don't they, and it rains out there once in a blue moon. Do you reckon we ought to start building that raft?'

Gerald's eyes were troubled.

'Or do you think we should start walkin' round the island? It looks a pretty big place, Gerald. It might be all right farther on.'

'I reckon the settlement down there scotches that idea. I reckon they built it the best place they could find. Anyway, I said we can't.'

'Everyone else says we should. And if we don't move off mighty soon we won't be able to. We've got to think of Jan and Colin. They were awful sick yesterday.'

Gerald pulled a face.

'They lost the lot! They must feel worse than we do. and we've *got* to find water.'

'Do you reckon we could drink the sea?'

'*All* of it?'

'Oh, grow up.'

'You can't drink sea-water, Gerald. You know that. They reckon it kills you or drives you mad or something. I reckon we've got to shift somewhere else or sling that raft together while we can.'

'Build a little one if you like and put it to sea with a note on it. That might do some good.'

Bruce grunted.

'Not a bad idea really,' Gerald said, warming to it. 'Write it on a hanky or something; one of Carol's with Carol's lipstick. Better still, build half a dozen of them and shove them all off to sea with notes on them.'

'Yeh, and then wait for fifty years for someone to find them.'

'Well, if you're going to take that attitude –'

'It's no different from what you're saying about a big raft, Gerald. Honest, it's not. We've just got to build it!'

'No.'

'Why not, for Pete's sake?'

'I've told you.'

'Look, all this talk about dying's not so stupid. How long can you last without water in a hot place like this? Not long. Not long enough for notes to find their way across the ocean. Golly, Gerald, we could be dead by tomorrow.'

'Where's Carol?'

'Oh, I don't know.'

Gerald gave a heave on his wing section and Bruce trailed after him. 'We could be dead by tomorrow.'

Gerald suddenly wailed, 'I know. I know.'

Carol, with a good stout stick in her hand, had walked inland a way, skirting the marshy land. The stick had a knobbly root on the end like an old-fashioned walking-cane. Perhaps she had walked a mile, perhaps two miles.

She didn't stop until she was sure the others would never see her, nor find her either, even if they came deliberately looking. The earth was still sandy, even way back here, and endlessly undulating, but with undulations rarely so deep that her visibility was shortened. The vegetation was brittle-looking stuff, and sparse, and it wasn't difficult to find a clean piece of ground to lie on, though first she took the precaution of carefully looking around. Once or twice she had looked back and seen Gerald or Mark, but that hadn't happened for a while. Then she got down, flat to the earth, closed her eyes, and waited.

She tried to think back to years long before she was born, back 100 years, back 200 years to the unwritten days before white men had come. It was a picture that formed easily enough. In different places she had seen the things that made up the picture; all she had to do was bring them together. And listen.

The wind spoke. Leaves spoke. Even the ground spoke. The ground had a beat to it, like a slow human pulse. It was probably the sea on the shore. Or did the earth have a heart, a great booming heart way down below, down deep? She thought of dark men and dark women and dark children sleeping in the earth. She thought of Jim sleeping in the earth. She heard voices and sighs in the earth and bare feet padding the earth; not real feet, the feet of ghosts. Even the years slipping back had a sound of their own, like wheels passing by, like wheels far away, drawing farther and farther away.

After a while, after perhaps ten minutes or perhaps hours, something seemed to click in her head. She awoke and the sun was no longer burning against her back. The sting had gone out of the heat of the day, but all the sounds were still there, above her and below her, and she felt different, unmistakably so. Comfortable, as though the earth had become a feather bed; rested and relaxed.

Her eyes opened almost languidly, and the earth was against her cheek, sand was in her mouth, the breeze was in her hair. Her hair had fallen over her eyes, diffusing her sight, lending to the bush a golden hue that did not belong to it. 'I'm still a white girl,' she thought, almost as though she would not have been surprised to find that her hair had turned to black. 'Do I know where to dig for roots? Shall I get up from here and find water? Has it happened?'

She didn't know, but there was a dreaminess in her. She felt slow and sleepy. So comfortable. She felt like something that had grown in the ground, that belonged, like a tree perhaps.

There was a pair of eyes, beady eyes she thought, looking at her. Two pairs of eyes on two long pendulous necks. Four long legs. Something stiffened in her, something went taut. Nerves and sinews stiffened.

Emu. Full-grown emu.

It was part of the emotion, of course, part of the picture she had thought up for herself. But she didn't move, didn't flicker an eyelid. She played out the part.

Where was the stick? Could she be swifter than they were? Could she stun a bird bigger than herself? Whether that bird was imagined or real?

'The emu is a curious bird.' She had heard that somewhere. 'When it sees something it has not seen before, the emu will stand and stare.'

Carol started trembling inwardly, from astonishment more than anything. The emus were really and truly there. And then she thought, Perhaps that's the way the dark people did it. Just stayed in one place, still and quiet, waiting. Perhaps you don't find animals by looking for them. Perhaps you lie doggo and wait for them to find you.'

The stick wasn't far. There it was. Probably within reach if she moved like lightning.

Then she said to herself, 'No good stunning it, is it? I've got to kill it. Can I possibly kill an emu, or will it fight back? I mean, how do I really kill it? Will it really fight back and will the other one go for me? Perhaps If I aim for a leg as hard as I can I'll maim it and bring it down, and then I'll have to beat it on the head. I'll have to hit over and over again, the way those awful men kill kangaroos, and it'll struggle and kick and cry out. Oh, the poor thing. Then it'll lie there all bleeding and dying and banging itself on the ground.'

Then she said to herself, 'And afterwards I'll have to drag it home, though I don't suppose it matters much if I can't. The others can come and help me. They'll say, "How'd you do it, Carol?' And I'll say . . . I'll say I was tired and went to sleep and woke up and there they were and I got up and killed one. "Gee, Carol," they'll say, "how'd you do that?" And I'll say, "I took a big swing at it with the club and killed it." "Gee, Carol," they'll say, "you, Carol; you of all people." "But I had to, didn't I?" I'll say, "I mean I *had* to. It was food. It was our life or its life, wasn't it?" '

She had begun to feel cold and sickened and afraid. But her fear was not of the birds; it was of her own clumsy self. She just wasn't made that way. She wasn't an athlete and never had been. She was clumsy at games; she'd never even mastered how to throw a ball properly. Not in a lifetime could she match an emu in speed or strength, emu that could run like the wind and slash with claws as big as hammers.

She remained there, breathless, trembling, peering out through golden hair into a golden bushland ruled over by two giant birds.

It was no use. She couldn't do it. She'd have to let them go away.

But then the others would say to her, 'You didn't even *try*? Oh, Carol. All that meat. We could have lived off it for a week.'

She shot out a hand, wildly and frantically, and threw herself to her feet, and in that instant the birds bristled and reared six feet high.

She slung the knobbly stick with all her might but missed by yards, and in seconds too short to recall they were gone on long, loping strides.

She stared after them, angrily, humiliated, until the

bushland was empty and silent again. Until long after that, she stood there.

Mark reeled down the sand with a load of sticks twice the size of himself. 'For crying out loud,' Gerald exclaimed. 'What are you building? A house for the little pig?'

Mark dropped his sticks in a heap. 'Gee, did you catch a pig?'

Gerald looked appealingly at Bruce then scowled at the wing section he had dragged home. And Mark blushed and dropped his eyes.

Colin was on his way back, too, apparently with an armful of shells. He kept on dropping them and wearily picking them up again. 'Mussels, I reckon,' Bruce said, 'he's been chipping away at them for hours.'

'I don't know what we would have done with a pig,' Mark said, 'eatin' a pig raw would be real gruesome ... It's a beaut house though, Gerald, isn't it?'

'It might be if it had a roof on it.'

'Well, that's something it won't be getting,' Bruce growled, so deliberately that he sounded his 'g's. 'He'll be wearing out the tomahawk on sticks. We should be keeping it sharp for things that matter.'

'Like what?' piped Mark.

'Like that raft.'

'By golly,' Gerald said, 'you take some convincing!' He sounded hearty enough, but didn't feel it, and got away from the problem by stepping through Jan's doorway of sticks. He was frightened of the raft idea because he knew it was his duty to fight it and he wasn't top-boy any more. Too many were against him. And the only weapon he had was argument, and so often he was weak in argument. Bert, the taxi man, tied him up in knots, and at the moment there was something about Bruce that was something like Bert. That same argumentative streak that always got Gerald rattled in the end. ('Steer clear of them, son,' his father had said.) So Gerald turned his back on it and had found Jan at her fireplace before he remembered that the same streak, in even stronger measure, ran through her.

She looked up at him, flushed and dishevelled, surrounded by her collection of fire-sticks that wouldn't burn. 'I can't,' she panted, 'the rotten thing. It just *won't* and my hands are so *sore*.' She turned them up to him, with several blisters formed and one blister broken. 'I've tried and tried.'

She was close to tears and Gerald felt awkward and wished he had gone somewhere else.

'If we can't start a fire, Gerald, we can't stay here. We can't eat raw any of the food we're going to find around here. We just don't know what those people died of. It might be something in the ground, and the water'll need boiling even after we find it. We've got to light a fire or build a raft. One or the other. While we're strong enough.'

Even when they weren't looking for a fight but just looking for sympathy it ended up on the same note, though Gerald's attention hadn't been entirely with Jan; he had been staring at a little perfume bottle, probably Carol's, that had obviously failed to make fire along with everything else, along with all the different sorts of wood, the flat sticks and the grooved sticks, the soft ones and the hard ones, that Jan had tried in every possible way. Even the green bottle that looked so old it might have come out of Noah's Ark.

'Where'd you get the bottle?' he said.

Jan sighed. 'Mark found it.'

'There might be more!'

'What good would they be, for heaven's sake?'

'For notes. Golly, Jan; notes. There might be dozens of bottles if we really look for them. That'll be better than any raft. We can do a circuit round the island chucking them into the sea every couple of miles. We can have them drifting out to sea all round us in every direction!'

Colin came in, wind-burnt and sunburnt, pink from head to foot, pink pants and pink skin, with Bruce and Mark at his heels. (Mark saying, 'Gee whiz; you'll be sore.') He spilled a heap of shellfish at his feet and said, 'We won't die, anyway. What else have we got?'

'Nothing,' said Gerald, 'unless Carol brings something back.'

'Crikey,' said Colin. 'Nothing at all?'

'Not a bloomin' thing,' grumbled Bruce. 'It's crazy staying here. We can't live on those things. Be like eatin' slugs or worse. They're probably poisonous.'

'Cockles poisonous?' cried Colin.

'Who said they were cockles?'

'I did. They look like them, don't they?'

'I don't know. Never seen a cockle except in a bottle.'

Gerald said, 'Mark found a bottle, didn't you, Mark? I reckon we ought to put a note in it and push it out to sea.' (Mark's eyes lit up.) 'Then tomorrow we should see if we can find some more.'

'I'll say,' said Mark enthusiastically. 'Yeh, I'll say!'

Jan pulled a face and Bruce said, 'We won't be here tomorrow not if I've got any say in it. And Col thinks the same, don't you, Col?'

Colin looked uncomfortable. 'In a way,' he said. 'I suppose . . .' Then he sat down and started cracking shellfish with the tomahawk.

'Don't wipe me off like that,' said Bruce, almost indignantly.

'I'm not wiping you off. You know how I feel. I reckon

we should go, but ... Heck, there are all sorts of things
to think of, aren't there? What if we do drift out to sea?'

'We're not going through all that again,' Bruce half
shouted. 'If we start thinking of everything that *could* go
wrong we'll sit here till we rot.'

'Better than rotting in the middle of the ocean.' Gerald
hoped to sound stern, but there was much more fear in
his voice than resolution. 'I don't know why you're so
stubborn. It'd be awful, Bruce. It'd be terrible. It's so silly.'

'I don't know what's silly about trying to help ourselves!'

'Don't let's start fighting again,' Colin said nervously.
'It's not worth it. We're friends; not enemies.'

'Yeh,' said Mark, 'what do we want to be fightin' for all
the time?'

'We're not fightin',' Bruce said sharply. 'We're talking
about serious things.'

Colin sighed half-heartedly. (Anything for a quiet life.)
'Well, I don't see anything wrong with putting a note in
a bottle; do you, Jan?'

She brushed the hair from her eyes with a self-consciously girlish gesture and went back to regarding her
hands as if they were part of a picture of absorbing interest.
They thought she was thinking about it, but in fact the
question had hardly registered on her mind.

'Surely you don't have to think about it,' Gerald said.
'It's common sense.'

Bruce drew a quick breath but Jan said, 'I suppose it's
something. Yeh, I suppose it's something. You never know.
Maybe pearlers or prawn fishermen or someone'll pick it
up. There must be ships out there somewhere.'

But she didn't really care; she was too much aware of
her own discomfort; of her hands and her thirst and her
deep, deep sense of foreboding. That they had actually

taken notice of her she didn't realize until the activity round about made it obvious. They had spread out a handkerchief on the suitcase and Gerald was writing the message with Carol's lipstick. They had accepted her word! *Her* word had settled it! Oh dear, surely everything wasn't going to depend on her?

Gerald wrote, '*S.O.S. Sea Wall Molineaux.*' There wasn't room for anything else. It was difficult making letters small yet clear enough. In a way Gerald felt thwarted, but he made the best of it. 'It'll do,' he said, and held it up for inspection.

'A real S.O.S.,' Mark hissed. He was anxious to be off to launch it into the sea.

'Doesn't make any difference what you say,' said Bruce. 'No one'll ever read it, anyway.'

Gerald made an impatient noise and poked the message in the bottle, then jammed a short stick into the neck after it, forcing it and turning it, bruising the wood. 'The water will seal it,' he said, 'it'll make the wood swell.'

'Yeh,' muttered Bruce, 'and then break the bottle.'

'Gee, Bruce,' said Colin.

Bruce didn't quite know what to do with himself. 'I'm sorry. I don't want to be a misery ... but crikey, I just can't see how we're to last the distance. We're too far away from people. We've got to help ourselves.'

'That's what we're trying to do,' said Gerald. 'Who's coming?'

Mark was immediately at his side. 'Let's carry it, Gerald. Let me throw it.' Gerald had wanted to throw it himself, but he gave it to Mark, and then one by one they trailed down to the water, even Bruce and Jan.

'Put a smile on your faces,' Gerald said. 'O.K., Mark. Chuck it.'

They stood there and watched it bob away on the receding tide but it wasn't exactly a moment of hope. The ocean looked so huge and the bottle looked so small; and the warm world of people and parents and places and streets and traffic seemed to be farther off than the stars.

16. The Golden Rule

The light on the beach had begun to change. Even the leaves of the trees were flushed as though washed in orange dyes.

It might have been dust still in the air from yesterday's storm in the south, or perhaps smoke from smouldering volcanoes far across the sea. Smoke could have come down on the tail-end of the monsoon. Or perhaps it was something peculiar to Molineaux. Perhaps it was like this every evening.

But it was strange (creepy, Mark said), like the light one might expect to find in a high and lofty place inhabited by spirits, where creatures not quite human lived. A beautiful light, but not ordinary, not naturally the way that light should be.

They talked about taking a swim to cool off, hoping that water on the outside might help to relieve some of the thirst on the inside. The boys, leaving the home beach to Jan, went across the headland to bathe on the other side. Jan seemed to want them to do that and assumed a frozen look when Bruce said, 'Aw heck, sis.' But they went, and going down through the rocks found a few fish stranded in pools, small brightly coloured fish as nimble as quicksilver that they managed to catch in a wild hysterical scramble with their hands.

'Are they poisonous?' Mark said.

'Don't be silly.'

'Black teeth,' said Mark. 'See.'

The tide was some distance out again and the sea was calmer. Farther out it looked almost glassy, becoming a brilliant mirror for the lengthening rays of the sinking sun. It made the water look hot, made it look like a sea of molten lava, as though steam and fumes and flames should have lapped at the shore.

Mark didn't swim, nor did Carol. Carol still wasn't back. Mark sat in the shallows and splashed himself over and when no one was looking took a big mouthful, swished it round with his tongue and cheeks, then spat it out again. He didn't know that the others had done much the same; Jan actually took one deliberate swallow. One only. Though she longed for more with a longing so alarming that she ran in fright from the sea. At once she knew that she had made a terrible mistake, almost a shameful mistake, for where matters of survival were concerned the others were looking to her. Not for any sound reason, not because she really knew more than they, but because she was supposed to know more. Bruce should have known as much; he had been a Scout for as long as she had been a Guide; but Bruce, the family said, didn't have a memory, he had a forgetory. When Bruce took off his uniform he stopped being a Scout. Though he said he did remember how to build a raft.

That was what Jan found herself thinking about now; the raft and the mainland and Gerald's idiotic bottle and *Oliver Twist* and the wireless set, too. That maddening little box with the big wide world locked up inside it, music and advertising jingles, rhythms and voices, all the familiar noises and excitements of the big wide world. That silent little box that wouldn't let the world come out. They had all sat there listening, waiting on that silent box to speak to them, pleading with it in a way, begging

it to make a sound, but it didn't even crackle. For two pins
Jan would have smashed it to bits. Maybe the others had
felt the same way.

'It's the batteries,' Gerald had said. 'The sea-water. It'll
never work; never, never.'

Jan was thinking about all those things because she had
swallowed salt water and hadn't lit a fire. She'd tried and
tried until she was jittery and frantic and her hands were
in a mess – as though they'd been burnt – but she hadn't
lit a fire. She'd tried the 'glass' from Colin's watch-face,
but it was really plastic and a bitter disappointment; she'd
tried knocking sparks off rocks; tried praying; tried everything; but nothing worked. The face of Gerald's watch
might have worked, but they couldn't get it off.

And there Colin had sat with his shellfish, his miserable,
mangled shellfish split open with the tomahawk. 'Well,
we've just got to eat 'em raw,' he had said, and so they had
eaten them, shuddering. And felt even thirstier afterwards.

'Let's hope Carol will have found something.' Gerald
had said. 'Let's hope she'll be back soon '

That was an hour ago, but Carol had not come back.
They had called her name, but she hadn't answered. Then
they had taken their swim.

How far was it to the mainland? Jan tried to beat
through a fog of facts at best only half-remembered. In
what direction did it lie? Fifty or sixty miles away, she had
said to the others, but it had been a guess. It might have
been 100 miles or 200; ten miles or twenty. Perhaps from
some points on Molineaux the mainland might even be
visible. But how would they find out if Gerald wouldn't
let them go? Jan hadn't bothered, ever, to look for Molineaux on the map. There hadn't been any reason why she
should. Probably it wasn't even named on the map. There
were scores of islands like that; apparently without people,

apparently nameless, until something happened on them and their stories were dug up from the record books. Even in class at school, Molineaux had been mentioned only in passing; a teacher had digressed for a few minutes from the course of a lesson about sunflowers and other plants like them.

Could a raft be built quickly enough to save their lives? Could they rig sails and help it along with paddles? Could they locate the direction of the mainland and push off, say tomorrow afternoon, and travel most of the distance by night to escape the sun? They had to watch the sun. Bad sunburn could be dangerous. Colin, not properly clothed, was already burnt; not blistered, but very red. They had found a hand lotion among Carol's things and used that on him, rubbed it into him gently and generously until he had gleamed like a well-greased wrestler. Except for his bones sticking out. Not like a wrestler really. Like somebody already half-starved to death.

The boys came back again, over the headland, bearing their insignificant little fish; four boys in a line, one behind the other; Bruce still limping, Mark dragging his feet, and Colin looking frail enough to blow away in the first gust of wind.

Jan felt for Colin a sudden concern, a sudden deep anxiety, and felt annoyed because he was so thin. God hadn't been fair to Colin. It wasn't fair that he should be so thin when Bruce was so burly and Gerald so healthy. And in her mind's eye – in a moment that came without warning – she saw time move on, saw days pass away, saw as in a week from now the procession of boys coming again over the headland, but there were only three of them. Colin wasn't among them any more. Then she saw the procession come again, but another was missing; Mark was missing. Then only one boy. Then none. And not even the girls were there watching. Not even Jan herself.

It was like a dream – but her eyes were open – a dream as vivid as any dream that terrorized the middle of the night. First four boys, then three, then two, then one, and then none. And Molineaux silent again except for the beating ocean and the gulls on the short. A dead place again.

It was a premonition in broad daylight; the sort of thing her mother spoke about. She had seen into the future.

Oh, what an awful, awful thing. Not that they were to die, but that she knew they were to die, all of them, one by one, until she alone was left. She was to be the last. Odd, to be last; to be left alone. And then there would be no one.

Or was it something other than that? Was fate offering her a choice? The choice to leave or the choice to stay? For if they left, how could the procession possibly come true? Perhaps, rather than a premonition it was a moment of clarity, of clear thinking, that had shown her what the future would be if they stayed?

As soon as Gerald was in hearing – he was running ahead of the others – she yelled at him, 'We're going. I don't care what you say. Do you know what's going to happen if we don't? Because I know. I've seen. One by one. One after the other. All dead. That's what's going to happen.'

'Where's Carol?' he said. 'Isn't she back *yet*?'

'Blow Carol. It's us I'm worried about. If we stay here we're going to die.'

'Look, Jan, it's twenty minutes to six. Last night the sun set just after six and it was dark so soon. Golly, I was sure she'd be back.'

'Carol's all right. Don't be such a sook about her. She's always off on her own. She was off on her own this morning and she was all right then, wasn't she? We've got to start building the raft.'

'I'm sick of the sound of the stupid raft.' There was a wild look in his eyes. 'It's Carol that matters. She's lost. I'll bet you she's lost. Can't you people understand anything? Raft, raft, raft; it's all I hear.' Then he looked at her sticks standing up on end, defining rooms, and threw an arm at them. 'What's wrong with playing houses? Mark and you. Why not keep on playing it? If you lit a fire it'd be to the point. Girl Guide and can't light a fire!' He threw his little fishes at her feet, gaping fish, mouths open. 'Cook them! I'm going for Carol. I'm looking for Carol. If no one else cares, I do.'

He ran up the sand and she screamed after him, 'Poison fish. Black teeth. Poison. Boy; and can't catch a fish!' Then lost her breath and would have sobbed if Bruce and Colin had not been so close.

'Poison fish?' said Colin.

'Told you so, didn't I?' said Mark.

'Gee; venomous, like snakes?'

'No, no, no. If you eat them.' Jan slumped on the sand. 'I can't get through to him,' she said. 'Surely he must know he'll die if we stop here.' Then she looked at Bruce. 'I've had a dream. In broad daylight, Bruce; a dream. We were all dead.'

'From eatin' fish?'

'I don't know what from. Thirst, I suppose. I don't know.'

'Not from eatin' shellfish, I hope. Maybe that's what the Saints died of. Somethin' they ate.'

'I wouldn't worry much about a silly old dream,' Colin said. 'I don't think that makes much difference. I reckon we can all see it coming without dreams to tell us. I say if it's a raft we want, let's build it.'

'Do you, Col?'

'Yeh. I do. And to blazes with Gerald. If we get to the mainland we'll be all right.'

'Could be the same as here, though, couldn't it?' said Bruce. 'Gerald could be right.'

'Gerald's a nut and so are you. What's wrong with you? And after *everything* you've said? It's the Gulf Country over there. Ask your sister; she'll tell you. Teeming with everything. Water and all. Not a blooming desert like this. Coconuts and jungles. I've seen it on the pictures.'

'Well I say, start now,' Jan said. 'Let's start getting the trees chopped down. We've got to get off this island as quick as we can. Even tonight.'

Colin whistled through his teeth. 'I don't know about that. I reckon it'd be better if we took the tools with us and worked out where the mainland was first, and then built it.'

'All right,' said Jan, 'that's all right, but let's do it. Let's cut straight across the island to the other side. That's where the mainland is, I'm sure.'

'Why are you sure?'

'Because of the way we got here, across the water. There was no land out the other way.'

'We can't go without Gerald and Carol, though, can we?'

'Leave them here, I say,' grumbled Jan, 'suit them down to the ground. Then they can hold hands all the time '

'You're a character, you are,' Colin said. She disappointed him with her moods. 'You sure say some things.'

'Clucking round each other like a couple of lovebirds. It's disgusting.'

'Come off it Jan. That's not true. Are you jealous or something?'

'Jealous?' she screeched. '*Jealous*? I wouldn't be seen dead with him! The creep.'

That made everything awkward. Girls were different from boys. Having girls around was like being trapped in a bear-pit.

'What a shame the fish are poisonous, sis. You couldn't be wrong, I suppose?'

Gerald saw Carol a little distance away. He had been running through the bush in all directions calling her name, then suddenly there she was, kneeling in a hollow of the sandhills.

He was so surprised that he stopped in his tracks. She was digging industriously with a stick. He didn't like her doing that, not in that way. It looked funny. But he couldn't bring himself, not then, to intrude. Her actions seemed to be private, somehow.

After a while he ventured closer, with uneasiness, because she still seemed to be far away from him, removed from him by something more than distance. What on earth was she doing?

'Carol', he called, and she jumped sharply to her feet, dropping the stick, brushing down her crumpled dress with hands in agitation. Then she looked up to where he stood and seemed to be at a loss.

'What's wrong?' he said, and walked towards her. 'What are you doing?'

He had caught her off-guard. For the first time ever he was seeing her off-guard. She was quite a different person, like someone small and young and helpless. He scarcely knew her.

'I'm not doing anything,' she said, and dropped her eyes away from him.

'We've been worried,' he said. 'It's late. It's six o'clock.'

Then saw on the ground not far from where she had been digging a heap of little fruits, nuts, and the roots of plants swollen with juices, and a dead lizard. 'Gosh,' he said, 'What's all that?'

She was still looking at her feet. 'Things,' she said.

'To eat?'

'I suppose so.'

He peered at them as though doubtful of their reality. '*Can* we eat them?'

'Why not?'

'Where'd you find them, for Pete's sake?'

She made an odd sound and gestured with her hands, almost in apology. 'Round about.'

'But *how* did you find them, Carol?'

She started stammering and fell silent.

He peeled off his shirt and gathered them all into it, twirled it into a bundle, and said, 'Let's get back, eh?'

She nodded and took hold of the hand he offered her and went with him.

In a while he said, 'How'd you know where to look for them? I mean, it's black man's food, isn't it?'

'That means you won't eat it, I suppose?' She was breathless and he could feel her tugging through her hand, trying to disengage his grasp. 'Of course I'll eat it,' he said, 'that's a funny thing to say.'

'What's funny about it? You hate black people. You sneer at them.'

He dropped her hand then, like a red-hot brick. 'I don't do any such thing!'

'You call them dirty.'

'I don't.'

'You do.'

'What's it to you, anyway? It's no skin off your nose, is it?'

She walked on and he pursued her. 'What's come over you, Carol? I mean, if people are dirty they're dirty. Black or white; they're just dirty. People shouldn't be dirty.'

'You're dirty,' she said. 'Look at you.'

He was taken aback. 'I'm not dirty. I'm clean. I've washed in the sea. I'm clean.'

'Your clothes are filthy.'

'Well, is that my fault? What else have I got to put on?'

'I'm dirty,' she said.

He was becoming confused and distressed. 'I didn't say you were dirty. You're twisting everything round the wrong way. Gee, you're not dirty. You're the nicest girl I know.'

'I'm dirty and sticky and smelly.'

He couldn't find the words he wanted and his face screwed up in desperation.

'I've been grubbing round the ground like a black girl on my hands and knees.'

He burst out, 'Well, what's wrong with that? I don't know what you're getting at? You're not a black girl, are you? And I wouldn't care if you were.'

'I bet you you would.'

He let her walk on, then, away from him, and made no effort to overtake her again. She was walking into the setting sun, a black silhouette crowned with gold.

He saw the imagery of her silhouette. It was very striking and in a way it taught him something, though not the truth. Not the real truth. He would not have believed her even if she had told him.

On the beach they were ready to move.

'They're coming,' Mark called. 'He's found her all right.' He ran down to the others. Mark was glad to be up and doing (he hadn't been much impressed by the idea of dying), though he wished he could take the house along with him. He had got as far as making the girls' room and the boys' room private from each other with a dense screen of sticks. 'I can see them coming,' he said, 'but they're not walking together.'

'Don't tell me they've had a tiff,' said Jan.

They let her comment pass. Jan's tongue, at present, was too nimble to tangle with. The idea some people had about its being a man's world had never seemed less like the truth!

'We're all agreed, aren't we?' she said. 'He's out-voted. We're going. No matter what he's got to say, we're going.'

'Yeh,' said Colin. 'I suppose so. Though whether it's right to go now?' He shrugged. 'We've got to walk straight and it's getting dark. Maybe we should wait for the moon.'

'There'll be stars,' said Jan, 'and the moon won't be long. If we're going to get out of this alive we've got to be on the other shore by morning. The island can't be more than ten miles wide. It might only be five miles.'

'I hope so,' grumbled Bruce. 'I hope it's not fifty.'

'There's not an island in the Gulf that big. They're little islands. Knock out Groote Eylandt and Mornington Island and they're all pipsqueaks.'

'This place doesn't look too little to me. And you haven't got my ankle, sis.'

'Don't you start again,' said Jan, 'or we'll be wondering which side you're on.'

'There aren't any sides,' Colin said distinctly.

'That depends on your point of view,' Jan snapped. 'If it's got to be sides it'll be sides. I'm not going to stop here to die just because Gerald wants to be stupid. I've had a dream –'

'Oh, Jan!'

'Well, I have. And I was the last. I was left on my own.

You were dead – and Bruce – and Mark. You were all dead but me. And I was left on my own. Then I was dead, too.'

'Yeh, yeh,' growled Bruce, 'we heard before . . .'

Carol came down on to the beach closer to the sea wall, but walked on, away.

'Hey,' Colin called. 'Back here, Carol.'

She waved, but started crossing the rocks. 'Hey,' Bruce yelled. 'Back here. Don't go away, Carol.'

'Where's she off to?' piped Mark.

'To swim, I suppose,' said Jan. Trust her . . . '*Carol*,' she screeched, her voice breaking painfully, 'come back!'

But Carol didn't and Jan's irritation and the hurt of her dry throat etched fiercely into her brow.

Gerald came down at that moment and stood a short distance away. His bundle dropped to his feet and his hands went to his hips in nervousness. He knew that something was up. Light was going fast but he could see the suitcase packed and sense the air of unrest. He didn't really have to ask what was up. He knew. 'Well?' he said.

'We're going,' Jan said bluntly, 'whether you come or whether you don't. And the same goes for your girl friend. We're not going to die like a lot of ninnies just to please you.'

Colin cut in with a tremor in his voice. 'That's not so, Gerald. She's put it wrong. We don't mean it like that.'

'We do,' shouted Jan hoarsely. 'We do. We do. Don't we, Bruce?'

'Blimey,' wailed Bruce.

'Don't you dare back out. You said we'd stick together.'

'Look, Jan,' Colin cried, 'that's the whole point. We do want to stick together. All of us together. We want Gerald to come with us because we think it's the right thing. And we can't go without Carol. Golly, Jan. Take a grip on yourself. We're not going to settle it by screaming at each other. All we'll get by screaming is a raging thirst and a first-class row.'

Gerald felt very much alone, stranded without Carol, but screaming or no screaming, row or no row, they would not pass him even by force.

'There's nothing to settle,' he said. But there was a shake in his jaw and a weakness in his knees. 'We stick where we are. That's the rule. Look, your lives will be on me if you go. I might as well have killed you if you go. Don't you see? My dad's aeroplane. My mother's guests. You can't go. I won't let you.'

'I don't know about that,' Bruce growled. 'I don't know about this letting business. I'd like to see you stop us, that's all.' He didn't like himself for that – or for Jan's attitude either – not after yesterday, but today was today and it was different. 'We're cutting across the island, see, to the other side, then we're building the raft and heading for the mainland.'

'And how do you know the mainland's there?'

'We know. We've worked it out. With paddles and sails we'll do it in a night. Tomorrow night. Tonight even, if we get across soon enough.'

'You've *worked* it out? You've talked yourself into it, you mean. You've no more idea where the mainland is than I have.'

Jan started up, but in sudden anger Colin shouted her down, and Mark flinched. Mark didn't like the way things were shaping. He liked a fight, but not with kids as big as these.

'Shut up, Jan,' Colin had shouted. Then he turned to Gerald. 'You're wrong about it, Gerald. You really are. They'll never find us here. There's not a hope in the world.'

'You're the one that's wrong! They're not fools. They've had plenty of practice looking for people. People across Queensland must have heard us. They'll get round to it in the end.'

'Yeh, and what happens to us while they're getting round to it? I reckon they'll run a dead heat with this bottle idea. The bottles will never get there and they'll

never get here. On the mainland we've got a chance. We can grub around for our food even, if we're *quick*. But we've got to get there quick!'

'Oh, blow him,' said Jan. 'Why waste time with him?'
She made a grab for Carol's case and headed with it up
the beach straight at Gerald. 'Now stop me,' she taunted,
'let's see how big and brave you are.'

'No, Jan,' cried Colin. 'Don't . . .'

'I'm with her,' Bruce bellowed. 'Go through him, Jan.
Let's get it over with. If he lays a hand on you I'll flatten
him.'

Gerald backed away from it all, bewildered. 'No, Jan,'
he pleaded. 'Please, Jan, no.'

'Puff of wind,' she said, and walked past him, and but
for her sneer might have got away with it. Gerald's temper
flared and he grabbed a handful of her dress and wrenched
her off her feet. She hit the sand shrieking and he darted
back towards the trees and faced them again like a prize-
fighter, with his hands up. Bruce came lumbering for him,
forgetting that his ankle had been hurt, but he walked
into a fist that Gerald had never used before, that Gerald
himself had not known that he possessed. He unwound it
and flung it at Bruce's face and Bruce went down yelping,
with blood spurting from his nose.

'You won't go,' Gerald yelled.

He darted along the beach a few more yards and shaped
up again. 'Come on,' he yelled. 'One at a time or all
together.'

Bruce was getting back on to his feet, spluttering and
wailing. 'Me nose. He's busted me nose.' And Jan, still
sprawling, was flabbergasted. Not for a moment had she
thought that he would do it. Not for a moment had she
thought that he had the nerve. He'd manhandled her.
Thrown her down. And stopped Bruce. Stopped Bruce
like a wall. And Bruce had had enough. He was holding
his head back and pressing fingers to his nose, gasping,
reeling in circles, making the most of it. But Colin hadn't

made a move. There he stood with drooping shoulders, Mark at his side. Colin had no heart for a fight, not with Gerald, not when Gerald might have been right.

Jan was alone without a doubt, but not in the way of the dream.

'Crumbs, Gerald,' she murmured, 'you didn't have to play it so rough. It's not as if we hate each other or anything.' Then she picked herself up and went back to her fireplace to be on her own, and started twirling one pointed stick into the groove of another with savage energy, gritting her teeth because her hands were so sore.

She had Mark for company after a while, after perhaps a quarter of an hour, and he said, 'Carol's a queer one, isn't she?'

'Is she?' Jan said.

'Yeh. She's still out on the sea wall, just standin' there. Is she all right, do you think?'

Jan sighed. 'I wouldn't worry about her. I suppose she's upset. She had a row with Gerald.'

'Is that why you're upset, too, because you had a row with Gerald?'

She didn't say anything, just twirled the stick between her raw hands, perhaps with less hope for fire than to punish herself with pain.

'Will we finish the house tomorrow, Jan?'

'I guess so,' she said, 'yes, of course we will. Where are the boys?'

'Gone after the ducks.'

She looked up.

'They said I had to stay with you in case – aw, you know – in case of anything.'

'What ducks, Mark?'

'Bruce saw them when they were fixin' up his nose. They flew right over the top of him they did, going inland.

Ducks head for fresh water at night, Gerald says. Well, fresh enough, anyway. Fresh enough to drink at a time like this.'

She was crying, but Mark couldn't see that, and when she dropped her eyes again the point of the twirling stick was glowing in the dark.

'No,' she gasped, thunderstruck. 'It can't . . . It couldn't . . .'

'Yes,' Mark yelled. 'Yes it is, Jan! Keep it going, Jan. What do I do? What do we do, Jan? Tell me, Jan. Quick.'

But she had started laughing; sobbing and laughing.

'You silly so-and-so,' he screeched. 'Tell me what to do.'

She continued to spin the stick, sobbing and laughing and wincing from the pain in her hands. 'The grass, Mark. Put the grass against it and blow. It's in the fireplace. Quick, Mark.'

He grabbed it, a great fistful of it, and it crumbled like old straw and he was shaking so much that he couldn't get it in the right place until the second try and then he blew and almost at once smoke puffed, and suddenly flames came, singeing his hair, handfuls of flame that Jan, shrieking with excitement, pushed into her fireplace.

Then they sprawled away from it, licking their burns, still shrieking, and Mark started dancing in a circle with his finger in his mouth, making a noise like a Red Indian, flickering shadows and showers of sparks and bright smoke, and Jan, exhausted, lapsed into a smile, a set smile of something like bliss.

The fire leapt up, crackling, with a warm glow and just like an ordinary camp-fire that might burn in that other world where friends and families lived far away. It immediately brought that world so much closer, immediately made it real again. And for the very first time, Jan found herself hoping that the people looking for them didn't find them too soon, for really and truly there were so many things it would be fun to do.

Mark suddenly fell on her and tightly grasped her blistered hand. 'Gee, Jan,' he said, 'isn't it beaut? Aren't we clever?'